SOMETHING IS NOT RIGHT WITH NADIA CARA. She's become a thief. She has secrets she can't tell. And when she tries to speak, the words seem far away. In Florence, Italy, with her epicurean brother, professor father, and mother who helps at-risk teens, Nadia finds herself trapped by her own obsessions and following the trail of an elusive Italian boy whom no one but she has seen. While her father researches a flood that nearly destroyed Florence in 1966, Nadia wonders if she herself can be rescued—or will she disappear?

Set against the backdrop of a glimmering city, *One Thing Stolen* is an exploration of obsession, art, and a rare neurological disorder. It is about language and beauty, imagining and knowing, and the deep salvation of love.

ONE THING STOLEN

BETH KEPHART

CHRONICLE BOOKS
SAN FRANCISCO

FOR BILL, WHO EMBRACED THE ADVENTURE

First Chronicle Books LLC paperback edition, published in 2016.
Originally published in hardcover in 2015 by Chronicle Books LLC.

ISBN 978-1-4521-5213-4

The Library of Congress has cataloged the original edition as follows:
Kephart, Beth, author.
One thing stolen / Beth Kephart.
pages cm
Summary: Nadia Cara is in Florence, Italy with her family because her professor
father is researching the 1966 flood, but Nadia herself is in trouble—she has turned
into a kleptomaniac and she feels detached from everything, except for an elusive
Italian boy whom no one but herself has seen.
ISBN 978-1-4521-2831-3 (alk. paper)
1. Kleptomania—Juvenile fiction. 2. Obsessive-compulsive disorder—Juvenile fiction.
3. Families—Juvenile fiction. 4. Florence (Italy)—Juvenile fiction. [1. Kleptomania—
Fiction. 2. Obsessive-compulsive disorder—Fiction. 3. Family life—Fiction.
4. Florence (Italy)—Fiction. 5. Italy—Fiction.] I. Title.

PZ7.K438One 2015
[Fic]—dc23

2014005286

Manufactured in China.

MIX
Paper from
responsible sources
FSC
www.fsc.org   FSC™ C101537

Design by Kristine Brogno
Typeset in Adobe Jenson.

10 9 8 7 6 5 4 3 2 1

Chronicle Books LLC
680 Second Street
San Francisco, CA 94107

Chronicle Books—we see things differently.
Become part of our community at www.chroniclebooks.com/teen.

There are 400 billion birds in this world.
Every one of them came from an egg.

ONE THING LOST

I

If you could see me. If you were near.

This, I would say.

Here.

This is the apartment that does not belong to me. This is where I've come to. Florence, Italy. Santa Croce. The second floor off Verrazzano. These are the windows in the front and the windows in the back and the long grainy planks in between. This is what the owners, the Vitales, left behind: Their smell (mothballs, glue, tomato paste). Their winter coats and boots (bear backs and houndstooth). Their razors, creams, and gallon bleaches, their yellow butter tubs and Kool-Aid-colored flasks and wide-bottomed drinking glasses from which the ivy grows. Up the walls, across the picture frames, over a bridge of thumbtacks, that ivy grows.

See? I would say.

Here.

It is night. A piano moans. In the apartment above, someone lights a sweet cigarette. Puff clouds. Down in the alley behind the restaurant, the waiters smoke, and the cooks share a jug, and one of the restaurant girls is dancing in tall silver shoes. The moon is a lantern; I reach. Over the sill. Into the ashy air. Into the sound of that girl dancing.

Shhhhh. Be very still.

It is early September. Across the ocean, in West Philadelphia, it is not morning yet. In her round room, in the Victorian twin, my best friend, Maggie, is sleeping. The cats and dogs and the kids are sleeping, and the birds are sleeping, their heads on the pillows of their backs, their beaks tucked into their feather warmth, their ears alert, their wings ready. *Danger.*

Thoughts in a circle.

The moon out of reach.

There is a ship of stolen things. See? *There.* On the top bunk of the borrowed bed. Up the squat ladder and among the Barbie-pink sheets that no one sleeps in for now. An olive felt hat. A broken kaleidoscope. Those scarves they sell for three euros each in the stalls of San Lorenzo. Nuts and bolts and rope and thread and the larger half of a cracked doorknob. A sheaf of bark and a skirt of lichen and the jewels and sometimes (I can't help it) their satin pillows. Glass beads. Paper stamps. The garlic chains that hang from the hooks at the Sant'Ambrogio Market. The rosaries at tourist shops. The braided cords of leather. The hard things and the soft things.

I took them.

I had to.

Don't judge me.

I lean into the night and the moon. I lean out and away from the borrowed room—the little-girl drawers, the little-girl chairs, the bottom bunk where sometimes I lie, curled on my side, trying to think my way out of this fix, out of me. Once I dropped a pencil. It rolled across the floor and disappeared beneath the heating grille. I needed the pencil. Got down on my knees. Found a tiny locked diary, no key.

Someone has left her life behind.

I wish that you could hear me.

2

Night is gone. Dad is near, calling me from the other side of the
door, where he cannot see the splinters in my hands, the threads
on this bed, the spill of glitter, the artifacts of thievery, the one
fine thing I've made out of the muck I am. Dad doesn't know the
secrets I keep, and besides, how can I tell him?

Nadia, Dad says. Honey. *Please.*

There's hardly any light out there, in Santa Croce. Only the
thinnest streak of pink breaking the purple black of sky. It's too
early for anything and too late to have never gone to sleep, and
I am Dad's firstborn, his primo student, the one who always listened best to the stories that he tells: Nadia Cara, the professor's
daughter. But now when Dad calls to me my thoughts break into a
thousand scattering pieces, and I can't be who he thinks I am, and
that doesn't mean that I'm not sorry. I'm very, very sorry.

Nadia.

I climb out of the bunk, change, hide what I can. I stand near the open window and breathe—remembering a long time ago, in Philadelphia, when I was maybe nine or ten and Jack was seven or eight and Mom and Dad were saying, *Wake up.* It was the middle of the night. My eyes were full of sleep. Dad had my hand and Mom had Jack's hand and they were saying, *You'll see. It's worth it.* They led us down the stairs, out onto the porch, into the street. They wrapped us in blankets. They said, *Open your eyes,* and we opened our eyes, and we saw them. Missiles of white. Missiles of pink. Meteorite sky. We blinked. They vanished.

Nadia?

I open the door, lock it behind me. I see Dad down the hall, pacing like a big bear unhibernating. He walks as if one leg is shorter than the other, as if there's more weight on his heart side, as if he can get the sleep out of his head by combing his hand through his hair. He stops when he sees me. He smiles.

There you are, he says.

Morning, he says.

After you, he says.

I say nothing.

The door to the apartment clicks shut behind us. The stairwell lamp blinks on. We round the thick stairs down, past the smell of cigarettes, toward the Vespas and bikes that sit beneath the mailboxes on the building's first floor. Dad opens the door and the air of early-morning Florence hits us. The sounds of the microscopic trash trucks and the Laundromat suds down the way and the breakfast prep cooks at the restaurant, drinking their coffee on the street.

Toward the piazza we go. Past the white cutout face of Santa Croce. Toward the river and over the bridge—Dad wearing his professor trench and me in my sweater, my fingertip pulsing like a heartbeat. In the low river, near the dam, the egrets gather, white strikes against blue. On the bridge a pigeon flutters. The pinked sky is fatter now, and the birds are awake, and I remember something Dad read to me once about the flooded River Arno. How when it filled with broken things—trees, bridges, mirrors, paintings, wagons, houses—it looked like it had been nested over by a giant flock of herons.

My mind is a nest built by herons.

My thoughts are broken things.

We walk the low streets of the Oltarno—pass the street sweepers, the window dressers, the bakers. We walk until the mountain is on us—the long slant up. Dad is talking about the Arno now, talking about his project, his big book, the reason we've come to Florence. My professor dad. His sabbatical year. His words go in and out and the mountain tilts up and now something pink vrooms by—speed the color of raw sky.

Here and disappearing.

Sonic and gone.

Something in my heart clicks on.

Go on, Dad says. Catch us some dawn.

He waves his hand at me, urging me forward. He insists. Like I'm still the four-year-old in ponytails who went everywhere her father went, across an Ivy League campus. Like I'm the six-year-old who stayed up late to listen to the stories he would tell. Like I'm the girl who sat in the front row of his famous lectures, *We have a special guest with us. My daughter.* Like I'm the girl in the street with a blanket for a cape, watching the streaking stars vanish.

I am not her, not hardly.

I am seventeen and trouble.

Go on. Catch us some dawn.

I take the steps two at a time, brushing the birds out of their trees. I hurry along the curve of Viale Galileo Gallilei and over to the other side and up more stairs until the San Miniato cathedral is right in front of me—crooked and painted and perched. A bronzed eagle lifts its wings. Cemetery roses bloom. A faraway steeple bell rings. A Vespa huffs by the cathedral door, a duffel bag hanging from one handle. Sonic pink.

The sun cracks the horizon.

The morning holds its breath like a miracle.

My heart does that strange little thing.

Shhhhh.

3

Did you see it? Dad asks.

He rests his hand on the stone banister, breathes hard. Two of the cats from the green alley have made it into the thin altitude and are scratching their beards against the church.

There'll be another—dawn, I say.

Dad raises his hand. Measures the distance between the horizon and the belly of the sun. Decides that he's two fingers late for the new day. Turns to look out upon his Florence. I wait for him to mention the Vespa, the pink, the boom, the click inside my heart, but this is not what he sees or says.

Lucky people, he murmurs instead.

The words he uses when he's looking at Mom or sitting beside her. When he's thumb wrestling Jack and Jack's winning. When he's pouring himself a glass of wine at night and leaning back into the couch pillows, some dusty old book on his lap. When he's watching the dawn crack over Florence with his once and never primo daughter.

His eyebrows are completely wild.

His eyes are green.

They do not see what I see.

I leave him thinking. I walk toward the dark shadows that fall through the open door of the church, pass the thrill of pink, the smell of smoke, that Vespa—and leave it standing there, unstolen. Behind me, I hear Dad open his book and turn to a blank page, which is every page, because in all the time we've been in Florence, he hasn't written a word of his story, doesn't have a single sentence about the broken pipes, the gush, the busted dams, the mold that he says grew like a skin over the city's past. Two months into his sabbatical, Dad's book is empty.

Worse: his daughter is me.

I'm trusting you with the truth.

4

Long. High. Cool. White. Green. The nave of this church is a huge stone cage of doves and pelicans, angels and eagles. Everything carved. Everything still. The air is cool and unsunned. The wicks in the candles are burning. The pew is hard. The stone birds stretch their wings. I breathe.

Shhhh, I tell my heart. Let this world be.

I close my eyes and my mind is a flock of herons. I breathe again and my thoughts are the nests I've built out of stolen things—the fabric nests, chain nests, and loomed nests that hide in the dark beneath the bunk bed at the Vitales'. Nests the size of my palm and the size of a bucket. Nests the size of a bowl, the size of a drum, the size of the tubs where the ivy grows. They are one by one, wide and narrow. They are sticks and jewels. They are loose and tight. They are unbearable, beautiful, mine alone, my secret, my confession in the long, high, cool, white, green.

I hope you can forgive me.

A monk is singing, fitting his words into a single note. It is the sound someone makes when he thinks he is alone, and now I remember a day, two summers ago, when Maggie and I were out walking. We'd gone to the Woodlands, the old cemetery on the city's edge. It's hilly and it loops. Its graves are built into the earth or they are little granite houses or they are stone tablets, planted. The Woodlands was somebody's garden once, but now it's where the dead live and the roots of the old trees grab at the dirt, and where sometimes Maggie and I go when we want no one to know where we are. Two summers ago, Maggie and I were walking the Woodlands. We were coming up with our big life plans—who we'd be and how we'd get there because we were fifteen years old and professors' daughters and we'd been planned for and planning for our whole lives long, and we each would be famous; that was sure. Maggie, the archaeologist—off on a dig somewhere with a toothbrush and a shovel. Me, the historian daughter of the famous historian—like father, like daughter, like me. Everything for the two of us was preordained. We were smart kids, on the way toward where we were going.

Shhhh, I told Maggie. *Listen.*

Because somebody was high up, above our heads, singing this sad gospel song. Somebody was there in the garden of the dead besides the two of us. We saw the laces first, dangling through the leaves. We saw a long silver ponytail dangling, too, and the bill of a blue cap, and then, stretched out the long way across a limb, we saw the man himself—dressed in a navy-blue jumpsuit like he had escaped from some labor camp, maybe a prison. He'd pulled his cap down, bill to his nose. He sang like a bird sings, and Maggie and I stood in the shadows of one of those little granite houses and listened.

Leave it to you, Maggie said, after he'd finished his song and gone silent. After we'd slipped out of the shadows and started walking home.

Leave it to me, what? I said.

You always find the pretty things, she said. *Pretty is your future.*

This is what I'm trying to say, what I want you to know, what I want you to tell them when I am gone, because this bad thing is happening to me: Once I had a future.

I open my eyes, lean forward in the pew. I see the steps coming down from the balcony and the steps coming up from the crypt and all of a sudden the monk's song stops. Snaps. There are boots slapping the marble floor. There is a tattooed jacket whisking. There is hair like a lamp and a fistful of roses, and I look. *Look*: Someone is running. Rising like a ghost from the crypt. He flies up the steps and down the aisle, beneath the green arches, through the cage of birds, toward the patch of sun near the open door. Someone is running, red roses banging around in his fist. He's agile; he's brilliant, he's fluorescent, he's a boy—eyes straight ahead, until—just now—he sees me.

Sees me.

Bows.

Raises his fistful of roses toward me.

Waits for me to smile back, and I do. Waits a second beat, and now again he's running—taking part of me with him already. I turn and his head is the color of light. I turn, and he is gone.

Whoosh.

Vanished.

It's the monk who threatens after him, bald and thin. The monk who rushes an old-man rush—his song gone and his anger rising up the stairs. His robes flutter over the marble floor. His rope belt swings. His sandals creak. He's ancient slow; his hurrying is creeping. The boy has flown through the cathedral door into the sun and the monk is barely breathing. The monk pulls up short at the door. Lifts the hand in the tunnel of his sleeve.

Ladro, he calls. Thief.

Cesare!

But the boy is gone. I hurry down the aisle, through the door, to the piazza. I search for a sign of the disturbance. It's only Dad out here by the wide rail with his empty book, a startled look on his face.

Nadia? he says.

I answer with nothing.

5

You all right? Dad asks again.

He presses his hand against my forehead. He tests for a temperature, the one thing he has always thought to do, no matter what, no matter where we are or how old I am, but this is the thing: Fever is not the name of my disease.

Someone was—running, I say at last.

You, Dad says. You were.

No, I say. I mean—Someone else.

Dad smooths his caterpillar eyebrows. He gives me a long look and I give him a long look back and all I see in his two green eyes is a narrow girl: me. She has black hair and her mother's bones and a big fringe of lashes and behind her the Vespa is gone, the pink duffel bag, the boy, the monk, the song. The rose hello.

I saw nothing. Nadia. No one.

In the city the sun is higher than it was. The towers and the squares and the roofs and the facades are browns and yellows, whites and greens. Birds are cutting the sky—swooping low and high. Florence is down there, and so is Dad's river, and so are Mom and Jack and the person I'm supposed to be. The boy must be down there, too, and that Vespa and that streak of pink, and now petals are flicking off with the breeze—petals like butterfly wings, like snow.

Red rose petals.

Nadia? Dad says.

But I'm already gone; he cannot stop me. I'm down the steps, along the curve, hurrying. The first dropped petal feels like nothing in my hand. The next is silk. The third petal fits, like all the others fit, into my palm. Petal. Petal. Petal. Soft red sweet. My hands grow fat with the color of red, which does not weigh a thing.

I pass the cats; I pass the tourists. I pass the stones and the bugs and the trees. I leave the altitude inch by inch, make my way into the city. Far away, Dad calls to me—tells me to wait, to stop, what are you doing, Nadia? But the steps draw me down, the streets draw me in, the red and the promise of pink. I go into the alleys, past the shopkeepers, turn back. If there was a boy (and didn't you see the boy?), he's altogether vanished. It's only my father on the hill behind me, his journal in one hand, his eyebrows rearranged by the breeze.

Like somebody had you on a string, Dad says when he finally catches up to me, when he can breathe. Down all those stairs, he's come. Into the alleys. Through the streets. The breeze in his hair. My old, lopsided father.

He glances out across his city. Shakes his head, very slow. Loops his arm through mine, like an anchor. Studies me hard.

You look a little . . . He searches for the word. Mesmerized. Is there something . . . Are you . . . ? You sure you're all right?

There are two of me in Dad's eyes. There's a line of worry in his brow. He locks his arm tighter into mine and waits for me to explain, but I already have, best as I can. *Someone was running.* Dad waits for more. There is nothing more.

I'm doing the best I can. See?

How about we not mention this to Mom, Dad says finally, and I nod. How about we—? he starts, then stops, and now we walk— over the bridge, past the crowds, around the corner, beneath the statue of Dante, across the piazza, all the way to Verrazzano—his arm hooked in my arm, his heart too heavy on one side. We walk to the borrowed flat on the borrowed street, past the stink of old air and motor oil.

Up the stairs.

All right, I think. All right. All right.

Tell me I'm not crazy.

6

Spiceologist at work, Mom says when we open the door to the flat.

She goes tiptoe in her bare feet to kiss Dad on the cheek. Touches her hand to the tornado of his hair. Points at Jack like he's a game-show prize.

Behind Mom Jack lifts one hand in a hello salute without looking up from the kitchen table, where he's got his spice jars out, his tablespoons, his whisks and bowls, like some medieval experiment. His hair spikes through his Skullcandy headphones. There's a dark dot of fuzz on his chin. He wears the plastic apron the Vitale family left behind—the one with pictures of the Duomo stacked up in columns and rows, versions of purple and yellow.

Zuppa di cozze con fagioli borlotti, he says. Hot mussel soup.

It's the Day, Mom says, of the Chili Pepper.

Dad touches his hand, briefly, to Mom's waist. He looks at me. Smiles at her. Stands there lopsided, his empty book in his pocket.

Jack slides a headphone off one ear, gives us a mealtime update. He puts the music back on and waves his hand above the page in the Marcella cookbook that he's been working from. Marcella Hazan, the queen of Italian cooking, is Jack's idol. This is Almost Independent Study 101—the recipes Jack's been cooking through to get his science credits for Friends High. Mom got the school to approve the scheme. Jack calls it his fair trade, since everything he loves is back there in Philly and only his own fine cooking ranks as a sufficient consolation prize. He's rinsing the mussels now. He's soaked the cranberry beans. Plum tomatoes sit in a bowl, drowning in their juice.

Amir called again, Mom tells Dad.

And?

Trouble, Mom says. I told him he has to see it through.

She crosses her arms like she does when she talks about her at-risks: the kids who need her wherever she goes, the kids, she says, who keep her young, and she is young, in those blue pants with the wide waistband and the little white T-shirt that she irons. Her dark hair streaks cinnamon. Her arms are yogi-thin. Amir's her toughest case, the kid she didn't think she should leave behind, and now Jack looks up and hands Mom a fresh bowl, a sharp knife; Jack always knows what to do. Like Thanksgiving eve, a year ago, when the news about my uncle Mike came in—wrong splurge of blood in his brain. *He had the worst jokes,* Jack kept saying. *He gave us the stupidest gifts.* Which is what we were going to miss most about my mother's brother—the stupid and the worst of him, his piles of wrong presents, the hiccough in his laugh. Mom kept cooking, she couldn't stop, the light coming in yellow and green through the stained glass of the Victorian twin, the roosters gawking, a spill on the white kitchen counter. She was banging and stirring and making. She was stuffing the turkey. She was sugaring cranberries. She was folding and pounding and finally Jack got up from the table and helped her sugar and fold and pound until something eased in her. Until she could cry out loud, with us.

You have a good morning? Mom asks Dad now, her knife working a steady rhythm in the small space beside Jack.

Dad squints like he's looking for something.

He lies outright for me.

7

When it's all done and good, all soaked and steaming, Jack takes the lid off the pot and delivers his lesson of the day: Chile peppers. History? Americas born, Columbus discovered. Medicinal value? Plenty. Influence on the mussel soup? Properly administered, Jack quotes Marcella, chile peppers "add spice with restraint." He lifts his spoon and takes a sip. He closes his eyes and swallows. A *MasterChef* wannabe. A TV star in the making. A kid without a secret. My tall little brother, Jack.

The spice jars are bouquets on the table. The pots and the pans and the whisk and the bowls and the tablespoons and the suds are stacked in the sink. Dad sits at one end of the table and Mom on the other and Jack and I sit across from each other, our bowls so big and the table so narrow, and they're talking like the Caras talk. News of home. News of the weather. News of Florence and Philadelphia—sister cities an ocean apart. I think of the boy. I think of the weight of the petals, which is the weight of nothing, the secret in my pocket. I think of what I saw and what Dad didn't, and all the tricks my mind plays on me.

Impressions? Jack is saying, I hear him saying, I listen.

Pungent, Dad answers, after a long think.

Jack slips his journal from his apron pocket and writes the word down. Seven letters. Substantial flourish.

An extravagance of basil, Mom says.

Notes of basil, Jack rephrases. Writes it down. The tip of his tongue poking through the O of his lips.

Nads, he says. Impressions? He holds his pen up in the air like a conductor waiting to strike, and I've got—nothing. I've got a brain like a nest, thoughts in a weave, red in my pocket, questions about the color pink. Jack waits. I take another sip of his mussels, close my eyes, concentrate. Do this, I think. Try. Open your mouth and speak. And suddenly I'm remembering Scrabble games in West Philadelphia. Adjectives, inflections, hooks, the racks of blanks and S's, my famous double doubles, the JQXZ that I could always blitz, and Jack kicks my shin beneath the table. Gives me a look: a big don't-fail-me stare.

Yo, he says. Earth to Nadia.

Good, I say, at last.

Good? Jack throws himself back against the chair. Good? For Marcella's mussels? For *chiles*? That's it? Jack looks at Dad who looks at Mom who looks at me and bites her bottom lip for half a second.

Giving you a pass on impressions, Jack says now.

Mom tucks a strand of hair behind one ear and looks again at Dad. Jack puts his pen and his journal back in his pocket and rubs the dot of hair on his chin. The talk starts again, a quiet circus. I stand up, very quiet now, my bowl shaking in my hands.

Feeling really—tired, I say.

Honey? Mom asks.

Just. Need a little—nap.

It's early afternoon, Dad says. The day has only half started.

Mom reaches up, touches her hand to my cheek. Dad lifts one hand to his heart.

Really good, I turn and say to Jack. Really—good, Jack. I swear. You're a—master.

You need anything, sweetie? Dad says. From us?

I shake my head no.

Anything we can get you, anything you want?

No.

Okay, then, Dad says.

But it's not okay.

The boy, I think. What would he do, if he's real, if he's true?

What would he do?

What would you?

8

Don't say a word.

Hold out your hands.

See?

The petals soft as down and red as blood and real. I've glued one to one to one and dipped the edges into gold and strung a stolen tassel from the bowl, and what was lost is found, what was fractions is whole, what is beauty is perfectly strange.

See?

What is the name of this disease, the name for the girl who builds nests with stolen things, who sees what others do not see, who can barely, hardly speak?

Hurt like this is a terrible thing.

The night has come on. Through the window the darkness falls on the shrugging backs of the hidden courtyard. The loose screen door to the restaurant kitchen. The broken stones where the waiters stand. The butt end of the alley. The room where the bookbinder works among so many stealable things. Pretty papers. Spools of thread. Buckets of glue and glue brushes, a tick-tock watch—old, heavy thing. He keeps the lamp off, his shirtsleeves rolled to his elbows. Streamers hang from a rack above his shiny head in every nestable color. He works late as I do, obsessed as I am, and I wonder what he makes, and for whom.

This one's for you, I think, the words rising up from the past of me. *Gift for the gifted*. Old words, and suddenly I'm remembering Maggie in West Philadelphia, last October. She is pulling up to the curb by my house on Spruce, with the canvas lid of her Dad's Mustang down, her candy-apple hair blowing sideways.

The car is 1970s vintage and Maggie-style—the seat belts buried in the foam of the unstitched seats, the up and down of the windows only working on one side, a pile of towels tossed in the backseat to clean up whatever mess she might get in, including the bird poop that falls from the sky. Hang a flag from the thing and it'd be its own parade, and here's Maggie.

Where are we going? she asks when I climb in.

She has the wheels. I have the ideas. That's how it is.

She ties a straw hat to her head with a pink ribbon. She wears a green sundress, a yellow sweater, and a pair of boots a la Cher.

East and south, I say. *Queen Village.*

She drives. Through West Philadelphia, across our river, all the numbers of the streets going backward until finally she stops and parks at the city's east edge, leaving the Mustang open to the sky. Stands beside me hooking her arm into mine.

Now where? she says, *oh, Plan-ess.* Which is like Goddess, only smarter.

Here.

We walk south toward the Village, past the little restaurants and the shops. We walk and Maggie tries to guess the name of the adventure.

Ice cream.

No.

Thrift shop.

No.

Gargoyles and phonographs.

Not today.

What, then?

You'll see.

She throws her head back and laughs.

We walk and we talk and we gossip. We discuss, like it's thesis-worthy, the things we're supposed to be and supposed to do as the professors' daughters we are, the two best friends who skipped high school in favor of taking classes with the under-grads. Early Matricks, we call ourselves. Our parents' idea of quasi-homeschooling, because they want the best for us. Take the classes, take the tests, get the state to certify. We'll never go to high school—not Maggie, not me. We already have what we need. Our future is a snap and a ping.

At a shop called Curiosities we stop. It's a redbrick trinity way off the beaten path, three slender stories tall. Its door is tall and narrow. We open it and the bells chime sweet. We step inside, and it's a brave new world—taxidermy and garden tools, glass elephant eyes, shark teeth on a string. There are the fine white bones of a coyote, the caverns of shells, the twisted horns of an antelope scratching at the walls, packets of seeds. There's a bat trapped in a frame, feathers in a basket, the wings of ladybirds, and a cave-bear tooth, and the aisles are crooked, and a live bird is singing in a cage, and Maggie takes off her hat and throws back her head again and laughs and we are the two most uninsane girls in the world.

Jesus, she says. *This is the best adventure yet. Why didn't you ever tell me about this place?*

Just heard about it, I say.

Just when?

Dad was telling Mom, I say. *A student told my dad.*

Leave it to you, she says.

We walk through splintered aisles, single file, Maggie holding her hat out in front of her very careful, very prim, so that she doesn't break a tooth, a claw, an eye. So that she doesn't make the stuffed partridge fly.

Impossible, she keeps saying, and we keep our arms tucked in close, we talk to the bird in the cage, we walk one behind the other. The back room of Curiosities is odd and lovely—plants erupting from glass vials and amber sitting in transparent tubes. The guy

at the desk has his feet up by the register. There's a card that says
DON'T PRESUME. ASK.

If you need anything, the guy says. Then he goes back to the
book he's reading.

Jars, baskets, shelves, drawers, crates and frames and a tray of
keys, like old prison keys, with mangly, iron teeth, and there's a coil
of stairs—metal and thin, and we climb them up to the second
floor and we stop, and Maggie catches her breath.

Because the entire back wall is tinted yellow glass. The roof
is glass and light. From vents a breeze is being blown up into the
room, and from the ceiling, from hooks, from strings, hang the
wooden heads and arms and legs and nobs of marionettes. Jesters.
Angels. Clowns. Woodsmen. Old ladies with hooked noses. Car-
penters. Sprites.

World's greatest miracle, Maggie says, reaching up and brushing
the beeswaxed feet with her hands. She touches the hems of the
skirts, the funny noses. Our heads tilt. The puppets dance.

How can anyone make anything this lovely? she says, and we stand
there wondering, the two of us, which hands made these, and how,
until I take an angel off its hook, lift its wings, touch Maggie.

This one's for you, I say. *Gift for the gifted.*

It was so easy, being me.

9

Nadia.

Yo.

It is the cool part of the morning. Flies buzz. Sweat runs in small rivers down my neck, my shoulders, into the insides of my elbows, and I don't know what time it is.

Just open the door, Jack is saying. For Christ's sake.

Another night gone.

Another nest.

I run my fingers through my hair, push the window as high as it goes, fan the stale air out into the alley, and I'm coming. I knock the scraps of things off my jeans, collect the scissors, plug the bottle of glue, tuck the new nest into the dark beside all the other nests I've built in hours I don't remember. The museum of the beautiful and strange.

I unlock the door, crack it this wide, slouch into the hall, shut the door. Lock it. Jack stares at me through the shag of his hair, plays with the Skullcandies that he wears around his neck like a choker.

You building a bomb or something? he says.

I shake my head.

You at work on government secrets?

Could you—not?

Look at you. He leans toward me and pulls a strand of tassel thread from my hair, flicking it back and forth, like a pendulum. He tells me I smell like a factory. That I've been locked in my room since yesterday, and now it's nine-thirty a.m. It's the Day of Chives.

Down the hall, Mom watches with her at-risk eyes.

So? Jack says. You coming?

He goes into his room. Comes back with his Lunar Sprints tied on—silver and yellow. He grabs his keys and some euros from the dish that Mom and Dad keep on the counter—his Almost Independent Study account. I don't know what is next, where I am going, what will happen soon, if Florence is still raining petals, if this day will be less strange than the days that have come before, if the boy is out there.

Coming, I manage, and Jack wrinkles his nose.

Talk like a human being, Nadia.

10

Lunch of the day: *Sugo di peperoni e formaggio caprino.* Ingredients: chives and peppers, cheese and pasta. Destination: San Lorenzo— river of leather and silk and chutney and spice. The high-in-the-sky birds circle the lantern of the Duomo. Jack hurries ahead. I lose him and find him and lose him, and there he is, with a fat sack of stuff in his hands and a funky look on his face.

What?

The splendiferous beauty of spices, he says.

He turns back, looks over his shoulder. In the back of his jeans, rising up from the pocket, is a dash of green feather, the color of limes.

I lose him, I find him again.

Jack?

We walk and the streets are broken. We walk in the shade, but sometimes the sun. We go down thin streets to wide streets and cross streets, and we reach the square and stop. This is the Piazza della Signoria. These are the crowds. Huddling by the fountain. Standing in the arcade. Sitting at the tables of the outdoor restaurants. On the upper floors of the Palazzo someone has left the windows open and I tip back to get a look at the ceiling frescoes, the tapestries, the stones, the wax, the painted flying birds, stuck in their brushstrokes. I tip back to breathe and think of Maggie and me, on our backs at Clark Park, looking up at the sky after a picnic. She'd brought snapped peas and zucchini bread. I'd brought peanut-butter-loaded Tollhouse cookies. It was a good day. We were half asleep. A squawk of hawks flew by.

Did you see it? I asked her.

Absolutely, she said, and now she was singing Penn's Quaker song, and I was singing, too:

Come all ye loyal classmen now
In hall and campus through,
Lift up your hearts and voices
For the Royal Red and Blue
Fair Harvard has her crimson
Old Yale her colors too,
But for dear Pennsylvania
We wear the Red and Blue.

We were best friends. The hawks were actual. She saw what I saw. I wasn't crazy.

Jack switches his sack to his other shoulder. He looks toward the elevated stage, where boys and girls are sitting on folded chairs, pulling instruments from cases, blowing air through oboes. They test their horns and saxophones. They whisk the skins of drums. A conductor in white shoes, jeans, and a blue T-shirt raises his baton. The crowd lifts its arms like periscopes. Cameras click. It starts—Beethoven's Fifth—and we are caught in it. Sewn into the crowd.

I watch the Palazzo Vecchio through its open windows, the birds in their brushstrokes. I look at Jack, that smile on his face—MasterChef, the splendiferous spices. The kids on parents' shoulders clap and my mind goes in and out, lost and found, a strange and terrible beauty, and I remember another day with Maggie, in West Philadelphia, the two of us taking photographs of glass, reflections of glass, glass through glass, shattered glass, glass shattering.

Snap.

I hear a shout from across the piazza and turn.

Everything is now.

Cesare! Ladro!

It's the boy running like a blaze touched off, the boy on the far edge of the crowd. I swear it. See? His bright hair zips. His pink duffel roars. He is fast, blinding, turning the corner on the crowd. He turns again, and now when he looks back over his shoulder he smiles so specifically at me, then takes off for the river—past the Palazzo, past the Uffizi, in through the dark tunnel of the scaffolding ahead. I hear his bootlaces slapping the stones. I see the bright faces of purple dahlia in the open space of his bag. I stand and it's all over, it's done, it's not my fault or doing—my body pushes straight through the crowd. Something falls, topples, cracks. Something. Someone. My shoes run through the shadows of things. They slip in the scaffolding tunnel. They hurry across the stones of the street, through the honking of cars, through somebody yelling at me.

The boy is near. I am not crazy.

But when I reach the bridge there's nothing in the face of the river but a girl looking down: me. There's nothing except two dahlias on the ground. Dahlias, I think, for me.

What the hell, Jack says now, breathless, running up behind me. What the freaking hell.

Didn't you—

Didn't I *what?* he demands.

See?

What?

Him.

Who?

Him.

Don't do that, Jack says. Seriously, don't.

He yanks my arm, stops talking. Nobody talking to no one.

She just took off, Jack's saying. Running. Wouldn't turn around. It was crazy. *She* was.

Is it true, Nadia? Mom asks. What your brother says?

Not—

Excuse me?

Not *just*—took—off. The words like glue.

Dad is walking in circles. Mom is sitting with tea. Mom is standing up, then sitting down, and Dad keeps going. Into the kitchen, out of the kitchen, along the streamers of Vitale ivy. The girl from the third floor is playing the piano and now she's clopping around in her stilettos and Jack is flopped across the living room couch, until he gets up and unpacks his bag and starts washing the peppers, cutting them lengthwise, scooping out the seeds. He opens up Marcella's book, turns to a page, leans in. He looks up and across the room and back at me, thinks something, doesn't say it, raises his knife, chops one thing after another, square and even.

Even though your brother asked you to stop, Mom says. Even though you were knocking into people, could have been knocking into cars, could have hurt yourself, could have hurt others. Running after nothing.

Not—nothing.

Jack cuts the peppers into strips. He throws some butter into the skillet and chases it with garlic. He stirs, mad and quick, and looks up and shakes his head. Keeps stirring.

Two times in two days, Dad says now.

Two? Mom says. This happened *twice*?

I'll explain, Dad says. Later.

No, Mom says. Explain it now. I need the facts, Greg. What's going on?

I didn't want you worrying, Dad says.

What part of this am I not already worried about? Mom says, her voice so suddenly still that it frightens me more than anything she could yell. What part of this have we not already spoken about? What else is there?

Jack adds the peppers to the garlic butter. He flips them over, stirs. Mom looks from Dad to me, turns the earring in her ear, and except for the sizzle of the peppers and the garlic, the room is shush, and no one is talking, and I have nothing I know how to say. The boy was there. He left me flowers. They are hiding here, inside my sweater. I can't help what Jack can't see.

Lesson of the day, Jack says, very quietly, is chives.

Chives, Dad repeats.

I want to apologize. I want to say it won't happen again, but you were there, you saw, didn't you? There was a boy. He smiled. I ran. He left me flowers. He vanished. Jack didn't look up in time to see.

Say it, sweetie, Mom says.

But I can't say that I can't say. Which is one more terrible thing.

12

They eat without me. They leave me here, in the borrowed room, with the ship of steals and these sweet, dropped flowers, these things I've seen, these words I would say if I could speak them.

Listen to them.

Listen for me.

Not like her.

Some kind of phase?

I shouldn't have brought you all to Florence, we should have—

What else haven't you told me?

Nothing.

What do you mean: mesmerized?

You've seen her.

But what did she say when you asked her?

She said . . . she didn't say . . . You hear how she talks. You know what it is. Hardly at all, and then like molasses.

Yes, but.

I'll talk with her, love. I promise.

Gregory, I'm frightened.

I want to tell them everything.

I am afraid of everything.

Give me the words so I can save them. Save me.

Far away, and closer, they talk. All around, in circles. It is the Day of Chives. It is Jack's phone ringing, and doors opening and closing, and the upstairs stilettos, and now I hear Dad coming down the hall, his one side heavier than the other, and when he knocks on the borrowed door and I don't answer he does not walk away. He stands there, on the other side, saying nothing.

Tell him for me.

Tell him what I mean.

Please.

13

The moon sinks into the belt of clouds. The waiters, the cooks, the girls, the cigarettes, the bookbinder are sleeping. Even the girl on the third floor with the stilettos is sleeping, but I'm not sleeping, and my lungs are full of glue, and my fingertips are bleeding, but see, see what I've made, see who I am, explain me to me.

I wove dahlia stems into the bowl of the nest. I used the dahlia blooms as buttons. I saw the boy. He left flowers for me.

Beautiful.

Strange.

Outside the clouds are like snow. They are like back then, in West Philadelphia, another night in Maggie's room. Maggie's singing Joan Baez, a whisper. Her cashmere dress is mopping the floor. She has big hoop earrings on and a boy's tie like a bandanna, and her eyelashes are broom-bristle thick. *Dance,* she's saying, but I'm quiet and still on her beanbag chair, quiet and almost still, spaces between the thoughts in my head, and I am watching Maggie.

Maggie's style is Second Mile Style. It's the stuff she's rescued from the thrift shop four blocks down. The beanbag chairs that are lemon and mango and orange. The macramé banners hung over the foot of each bed. The shoe box in the closet where Maggie puts the accessories she has named for me: the Nadia choker, the Nadia beads, the Nadia feathered earrings. The two nameplates on the door that Mrs. Ercolani hammered in—*M* and *N*—like we're blood sisters, maybe even twins. Mrs. Ercolani is Maggie forty years from now, her red hair with stripes of white in the front, her eyes bright, and her happiest stories about the places she'll go, the places she hasn't been yet.

Hey, Maggie says. She's dancing. She's on the braided rug letting the vinyls spin on her Philips portable. She puts the needle down on Earth, Wind & Fire and rides the "Mighty Mighty" and now she's singing into the pokey end of her hairbrush and pulling me up with her free hand. I feel the bump of the song in my bones, the high rise of the old funk, the easy "Mighty Mighty," and the angel with the beeswax feet is dancing in her strings, her wooden knees clapping. Maggie touches her fingers to the angel's feet. She throws open the big-sash windows and lets the snow fall in. It's a snow-globe drift. It piles up on the sill and against the rug and Maggie sticks half her body into the night, puts her tongue out to taste the weather.

Through the open window the snow falls and the wind howls, and it's cold; the angel's dancing. *Don't move*, I say.

What? she says.

I have a plan.

I leave Maggie in her room, the snow piling up near her feet. I go down the stairs, past the big front windows, where the snow falls faster, plentiful and silent. It is erasing the streets and the sidewalks. It is frosting the bare branches of the trees and blanketing the gutters and all up and down the streets the lights are on and West Philadelphia is snow-cold amber. In Maggie's dungeon basement, stalactites drip and the washing machine rumbles and everything is damp, and at last I find what I came for—a length of rope. I take the steps up two at a time, find Maggie still singing, dig out extra mohair sweaters, one each. I unhook two striped scarves from Maggie's closet, dig out two pairs of thick socks, hand Maggie one, and all this time, she's just standing there, watching me, letting the snow fall into the room, a funky smile on her face.

WTF, she says.

No questions.

We pull on our boots. We're down the steps, out the door, we're calling to Maggie's mother, *We'll be back,* and now I tell Maggie not to move; *I have a surprise, close your eyes.* From the alley I pull a lid from an old trash can. I tie it to the leash of my rope. I blow some heat into my cotton-gloved hands, and the snow is so new, my boots sink in deep.

You sit, I pull, I say.

She raises one eyebrow.

Climb on.

She eases down. The snow deflates, lets out a crunch. I snap the rope and Maggie is thrown back and now forward, keeping her knees to her chin.

Some plan, she says.

Past the community garden, toward the edge of the Penn campus, between the towers, over the bridge and down Locust Walk. I pull and Maggie sits—the snow beneath us, our trail behind us, the snow falling. At the compass I turn toward Spruce and the massive Quadrangle dorms, where the street tilts and the building rises and from within the vast interior courtyards we hear the sound of snowball fights, laughter. Maggie's red hair has turned white. Her mohair shoulders and arms and the bottom of her dress are white. Her boots are white and she's disappearing into the night and the snow tumbles in and I see all this through crystal stars that have set between my lashes, through the melting of the night.

Then is now. Now is now. Everything is vanishing. Everything is disappearing. The new moon above Florence hides behind the belt of clouds and the first drops of rain have begun to fall, making splatters in the alley, leaving splashes on my cheeks. Somebody is crying. Through the open window I lean as far as I can and wonder what Maggie would think if she could see me now, what Maggie would do to save me, if anyone can save me.

14

Breakfast, Dad is saying. You awake? I hear him knocking on the door, sighing. I hear him rapping again until finally I open my eyes and everything is smudge and shadow and glue. Memory is steam. Dad's down the hall. I open the door, and there he is—his big linen shirt cuffed uneven at the sleeves and his khaki pants crooked at the seams. He has an apron on. It's a minute or two before he sees me, and when he does, he looks fake easy, like he's trying casual on and it doesn't fit him.

Breakfast, he repeats.

I slip into the chair across from his. I cup my hand around the mug of hot chocolate already on the table, and there are split places in my fingertips, cracks in my hands. I think of the dahlia nest, and the snow and the sled and the lamps in windows. *Focus, Nadia.* Dad piles French toast onto two plates. He grabs butter from the refrigerator, syrup, two forks, and he looks like a clown act, off balance, but nothing falls. He slides our plates into their places. He hands me a fork. He puts the syrup and the butter down between us.

Never made them so good, he says, about the only dish he's ever mastered. Eat some.

His tundra hair is sleep-smooshed. His glasses are crooked on his nose. He takes a sip of his own hot chocolate, cuts a triangle of sopping French toast, and lifts it to his mouth. Chews. Swallows.

Your turn, he says.

He says he has a new angle on his flood. Says Mom has made some progress with Amir. Says something about the lady across the street and something about the dog upstairs and something about a book he's read, and something about the weather, and now as Dad talks I am five or six or seven, and Mom is saying, *Let's go surprise your father.* She's taking Jack by one hand and me by the other and walking us down the wide wood steps of our Spruce Street twin house and through the leafy corridors of West Philadelphia until we reach the edge of the giant sleeping campus. We are a parade of three. We are young and smart, and the campus is silver and brick, moss and ivy, castles and courtyards, and at the far end of our forever journey sits the fine arts library, red and round and tall and chimneyed, something straight out of the Brothers Grimm. That's where Dad is—through the heavy notched doors and past the turnstile, in the massive reading room. It's a courtyard space with a roof four stories high. It is arches and arched sun. It's big books with thin pages and the smell of old things, cracked pencils, eraser nubs.

Oh, my loves, Dad says, *here you are.* As if we'd wakened him from something. My mom leans toward him and lets her long hair fall, like a screen between their love and ours.

Hey, I hear Dad now. Sweetie. Are you listening?

Dad leans back, stands up, goes for another slice of French toast, as if what I need right now is a fresher version of what I already have. He sails a slice of butter over the egg-white skin of the bread. Drowns it in syrup. Switches my plate for his plate, sits down, and waits.

You want to tell me what's going on? he says. At last.

I shake my head.

You want to tell me part of it?

I—can't. I—don't. Everything, I finally say.

Everything?

Is harder.

I hear my voice very soft and far away. I hear my words separating. I see Dad thinking, pulling his pen from his shirt pocket and snapping the ink tip in and out, his hands moving now, his fingers.

Is it?

Yes. Everything's harder.

I close my eyes, and it's dark inside. I wait for him to talk, to say something, to fix this, save me, but his words are far and I get caught inside his flood, a boat full of things passing by. Gears and gloves and bowls and scissors, the gold cylinder of a kaleidoscope and its broken, colored pieces, and silken ties and amethysts, the bright back of a moon and rose petals and royal dahlia and every nest I've made, every loomed cup, every whole thing, every infinite woven circle. Everything in the belly of this boat, on a dark night, on a Florence street, in the middle of Dad's flood. I reach for the boat and the vision shatters. I open my eyes. Dad's leaning close. Words like stones.

Honey, he says. What's this?

He takes one of my hands in his hands, turns it over. Ruby dots of blood.

He clomps down the hall, to the bathroom, opens and shuts the cabinet doors, comes back with a bright white box of Band-Aids.

Give me your hand, he says.

He wraps each of the broken fingertips. One by one by one.

I don't know what to do with you, he says, and so we sit there, the two of us, until the first raindrops come. Big splats against the windows, on the streets, against the white and pink sheets the across-the-street neighbor hung, into the sound of the morning. Jack appears in the hall, rubbing his head.

French toast? he says.

Have a seat, Dad says. Stands at an angle, making the toast, keeping a close eye on me.

15

The rain is sideways—big nails of wet stuff. The French toast smog is still here and the dark rain is out there and Jack's gone—left with his Almost Independent Study 101 euros in his pocket. Spice of the day: rosemary. Dish of the day: *Cappe santé con pomodor, agliog, e rosmarino.* Mom is standing at the window in her long nightdress, watching the street and the rain.

I hope he's somewhere dry, she says.

So much rain, she says.

Now Dad is beside her, his arm over her thin shoulders. She leans and she's so small and he's so big, a bear. The nails of her toes shine like lip gloss. She whispers and he whispers back, and then they turn, four eyes on me.

On the floor of this room is Dad's flood. All its pieces on note-cards, Xeroxes, newsprint. He toes the facts around—slides them across each other, looks for patterns and themes, looks up at me, expects *something,* because this is my Almost Independent Study, this is my work while we are gone—to be Dad's primo assistant, to collect the facts with him, and the dawn, to understand his flood. Fourteen thousand works of art. Sixteen miles of records. Four million books. Eighteen million cubic feet of debris. The big flood came. The city drowned. Parts of it were rescued. Find the start. My job is to help my father think in Florence. Nobody has to tell me that I'm failing.

It's been two hours, Mom says now, about Jack.

You kids, she says, and your phones.

She opens the window, puts out her hand. She says it's hard as hail out there, and I close my eyes, listen to the rain, the drumming on the scaffolding down the street, the slosh sounds in the piazza, the faraway cry of somebody laughing, running. A game in the rain in the street. The weather is outside. The weather is inside. It is almost sleep. I hear Mom walk by in her bare feet. I hear her come back, close now, the white whish of her long dress, and now I feel her pull a blanket over me, feel a kiss on my cheek.

Let yourself sleep, she says, but I'm already gone, remembering another storm.

16

It's Maggie's garden. Her split of land off Spruce Street—four feet by twelve feet, and a miniature red picket fence, a scarecrow, an old rain barrel flipped to make a stool. A storm is coming on.

Some of the other gardeners in this community acre have built canopies out of woven sticks so only part of the sun will fall through. Some have planted planks all around the edges of their plots, like coffins without lids. Somebody's put an easel where a garden should be, and on the brick face of an abandoned house are the flattening branches of an apple tree. Espaliers.

But Maggie's spot is the prettiest—the straw doll and the barrel and all these hand-painted signs promising: Peas. Clover. Zinnias. Tomatoes. Poppies. In the middle of everything is Maggie's fig tree, which we grew in a bucket on her porch until it was finally big enough for the Big Transfer. We bedded it down with straw a year ago. It's lasted the winter, and now it is March, and a storm is coming on. *Hail like eggs,* the weather guy says. Better batten down.

We work side by side. We undig the signs. We flip the barrel, unplant the scarecrow, lay a thick sheet of plastic down over everything and now we have to anchor the tarp with the broken plates of the sidewalk concrete that sit across the street in an abandoned yard. Back and forth we go with the weights in our hands, the dirty bits of broken sidewalk. Maggie's wearing her denim flares and her checked shirt and her garden clogs. Her hair is pushed back into a red bandanna and flapping over her shoulders in the wind, because the wind has already started to blow, and it is getting hard to hear each other inside the storm that hasn't happened yet. The skies stew. I stop.

Something in the fig tree has stirred.

Furry wings.

A mother finch, tucked down.

Maggie, I say. *Look.*

She is a brunette with a streaked breast coat. Her nest is straw and twigs, a patch of moss, bits of colored paper, and she is perfectly still until I get too close and she spreads her wings. She hops. She returns. Her eyes on us.

Three eggs, I hear myself say. *And it's only March.*

Too early for eggs, Maggie says.

The storm is coming—sneaking in beneath the tarp in the places between the concrete chunks. The easel that no one has battened has started to rattle. The branches of the espaliered tree are cranking from the brick. Maggie's hair is a red flag streaming, and mine is one black knot.

Nothing we can do.

Three chicks, I say. *And a mother.*

They'll have to ride out the storm, Maggie says. *The nest will have to save them.*

But a nest is only twigs, I think. It's only leaves and fragile things. The nest is so small and the eggs are so tiny, and the wind is blowing hard, and Maggie's saying, *Come on.*

The weather is hard and thick. It's time to leave. Between the plots of the community garden and up the street and past the mosque and Manakeesh, we run. Past the lady with the window boxes stuffed with pansies and around to Maggie's house, where Maggie's mom is waiting at the door with two identical towels.

You had me worried, she says.

I made some cocoa, she says.

We had to leave the—bird, I say.

We sit there, the three of us, listening to the storm. The rain first, and then the hail the size of eggs, and always the wind. I call my mom, tell her I'm here, and then the lights flicker and the power goes and Maggie's dad comes home and they stand, quiet, at the windows.

It rains all night. The gutters are full of things and the treetops are breaking. The fire-escape stairs bang against the brick behind the house and the trash cans are rolling, and everything inside Maggie's house is very still except for the trembling flames on the candles. We watch the storm. We stand in Maggie's flannel shirts and Maggie's sweats, no music on, no lights in the street. Maggie goes to sleep. I stay awake, afraid for the bird.

The storm breaks before the dawn. The candles run out of wicks. No clocks are ticking. Out in the street the big branches of trees are down and the loosened trash can lids are rolling around and pieces of wash that had been left out on backyard lines are lying on the ground like empty people. I tiptoe down the hall, past Maggie's parents' room, and down the steps in the squish of still wet shoes. Pull open the door. Step out onto the porch. Feel Maggie behind me.

Going nowhere without me, she says.

She wears her checkered gown over a pair of jeans. She's stuck a tiara into her hair. She hands me a shovel, a rake, a bucket, and we go, and we don't talk, don't say anything about the bird, about the plot, about the too-ferocious storm, and when we get there, the community garden looks like the end of the world.

The easel smashed into sticks.

The canopies smashed.

The espalier yanked away from the wall like a spider's web caught in a broom.

The planks between plots are down and the compost is sludge. Straw is everywhere, like chopped blond hair. But under Maggie's tarp the plot is dry, her scarecrow and her signs are dry. Up in the tree, the nest is whole.

The birds have survived.

World's greatest miracle, Maggie says. We sit with our butts against the soaked rim of the barrel and watch the bird come back to life. She spreads her wings. She settles.

We didn't have to worry after all, Maggie says.

And something in my mind breaks loose and almost free.

17

I wake up in the dark part of the living room. To Mom's quilt up
to my shoulders, another blanket thrown across my feet. The talk
is Jack. The talk is a girl. The talk is Mom saying, Shhhhh. Your
sister's sleeping.

But I'm awake now, and there's my brother beneath the halo of
the Vitale chandelier, bent over the kitchen table, slicing. I see little
trees of rosemary and fists of garlic and fat tomatoes and a girl Jack
calls Perdita.

She wears cabled leggings and a red mini, work boots and a
lace shirt with snaps on the cuffs of the sleeves, a navy-blue cami.
She wears her hair geometric—soft to one side, shaved on the
other, a dozen gold studs punched into the lobe of that ear. She
has fluorescent nails and a bold gold chunk of a necklace, green
feathers hanging like a pendant.

Bright green neon feathers.

She's washing scallops in the sink, patting them dry with a towel. She's jabbing a knife into the scallops' skin and washing again, patting them drier. Shows them to Jack, who looks up, says something, in Italian or English, it doesn't matter. Like they know each other well. Like Mom's lost the job of prep cook to this girl with geometric hair.

Dad's gone. The bits and pieces of his flood are gone. The rain is a quiet slick against the panes, and Mom is sitting in the chair across from me, dressed for the day and reading a book with her half-glasses on. She takes the glasses off, puts them up in her hair, puts them down on her nose, looks at Jack and the girl, reads, but not really. There's a huge umbrella in the hallway, little pools of water where Jack and this girl came in, and it's still dark outside, and wet, but the storm is over, and now here's Dad, opening the door, a bottle of olive oil in his hands. His umbrella is half bent, half folded. His wind hair is wrecked. His shoes squeak on the floor.

At your service, he says. To Jack. And I wonder how long I've been lying here remembering. How long she's been here. How well they know her—Perdita.

Beneath the blanket I slip the Band-Aids off, push them into a pocket. I watch Jack light up the skillet, uncork the oil and pour it, split the garlic into cloves and toss them. He leans over the Book of Marcella, scratches his head. He hands Perdita the rosemary trees, stands close to her, says, Like this. With his knife. With the rosemary. Not a spice, but an herb.

I feel Mom's hand against my forehead.

You slept a long time, she says.

Who—? I say.

That would be Perdita, Mom says.

18

She works the stall at the central market in San Lorenzo—spices. She is here. Real. No wonder Jack's acing his Almost Independent Study 101. No wonder he gets up each day and hurries to the market, to the spices, to her. Rosemary is an herb Aphrodite wore. Rosemary is Virgin Mary famous. Jack has a girl.

Blood and flesh. Sitting, not running. Real, and nobody's secret.

Around the Vitale table we cram. The leftover rosemary is in a coffee mug and Jack's masterwork steams from a center bowl with a spoon. Dig in, Jack says, and Mom sits beside Dad, who is holding her hand, like it's the most solid thing in the world, like she can't believe her son has this friend and has brought her home and then she looks at me and her smile dims.

Dad runs his fingers through his hair. Mom turns the wedding band around on Dad's finger. Jack serves the scallops, three by three, pours his sweet and garlic sauce, and he sits back, and there's talk, bits of English and Italian and something in between that I can't follow because I am thinking of the dahlia nest and its broken place and the chain Perdita is wearing. I'm thinking how happy Jack is with the girl right here, and how the boy is out there, waiting.

Someone was running.

Perdita's father owns the spice shop. Perdita's grandfather owned it first. They sell *senape bruna*, three euros for fifty grams; *pily-pily*, four euros for fifty grams; *pepe misto*, five euros for fifty grams; *peperoncino de cayenne*, four euros for fifty grams. The best spice shop in all of Florence. The family business, and Perdita works the mornings and goes to school in the afternoons, but mostly she goes to the school of spices, and she's talking about leaves and roots and gums and herbs and seeds, cassia and ginger, Marco Polo, and Jack raises one finger: Impressions?

Sweet, Mom says.

Jack nods, writes it down.

Dad?

Woodsy.

Woodsy?

Dad nods. Jack writes it down.

Nads? Jack says. Impressions? His voice all don't-fail-me, don't-embarrass-me, be a normal sister, please, and I take a good long look before I try to speak. Jack's hair is puffy from all the scallop steam. There's a bruise on his neck, a streak on his cheek, and he's a tall dude with this girl beside him, the sticks of her legs crisscrossed and her boots so big for her bones and her hair crooked and striped. *Don't fail me.* I look at Mom and Dad holding hands and the sticks of rosemary bouqueting in the coffee mug and I need a word. I need a Scrabble double double. One word for my brother.

Per—, I say. The start of it.

Jack leans toward me, the dot of the beard on his chin round and hopeful.

Per, what, Nads?

Perfect—ion.

Yo, he says. Yo, yeah. He high-fives Perdita. He high-fives Mom and Dad, and his smile is a bridge that runs from one ear to the other. Perfection, he writes in his book. Big and bold and underlined. Perfection: Jack's scallops according to Nadia. He looks at me like I'm the sister he's been hoping for, the kind who gives out props when the girlfriend comes home, and I stand up; that's it. Perfection is all I need.

19

I slip out the door in the clatter of cleanup; nobody sees. I walk where the buildings are the colors of skin, and the arches and shutters are the color of old rain. Toward the shop windows and the bank windows and the restaurant windows I walk, then walk on, until I am lost and far away and the only thing that can compass me back is the Duomo, its cap a lighthouse lanterning the way.

Birds are up high—thin black streaks. Kids are on the streets on bikes, and there's the tourist crowd, and there are bobbling balloons and rubber-ducky boots splashing in the rain that fell all morning. I walk alleys, bridges, riverways, circles, until I find myself at the Santa Croce piazza, where the puddles are catching the sun and the birds have come to rest on the head of Dante. Some skateboarders are throwing tricks off smooth boards they've laid down across the stones. They're riding and smashing and backing, their music coming from a tin box. One of the boys hits a ramp and whoops the sky and stops clean. One of the girls takes too much air and she flies, flies, flies, and I want wings, I want to crush the fear, the millions of things that make me afraid, the millions of things I can think but not say.

What do they mean: mesmerized?

What do *you* mean, when you say it?

What is the worst thing you've ever lost, and how in the world did you find it?

20

A shout from the east.

A bright, raw streak of pink.

In the piazza, on the fringe of the skateboard crowd, I see him. In the shadows of the outdoor cafes, in the margin places, the secret places—too fast, too quick, a zip of speed. It's him, hitting the piazza's south edge and running free. It's him with a clutch of sunflowers in one hand—too fast for the men on the chase, too fast for anyone; he is blooms and fire.

Hey, I say.

And he turns.

Wait, I say.

And he stops.

Drops a flower, bright and singed. Raises an eyebrow and winks. Runs.

Nothing will stop me. This is him, this is what I see: the thief, the giver of flowers. I cut through the crowds, go where he went.

Follow him toward the Arno. Through the shadows of the cathedral, into the narrow parts of the street. Past the gates and gelato shops, past the round stones of the *biblioteca*, past the coffee shops, toward the Lungarno. There is the whacking tail of a dog and the wheels of a wagon and a man in plaid, and the boy could be anywhere, but he's gone.

On the bridge the tourists are posing in the sun. At the top of the hill, San Miniato shines. Up and down the Lungarno the artists are putting up their stalls, putting out their tins, brooming the gypsies from the stone walk, and now in the other direction, between boots and sandals and flip-flops, I see a second flower, dropped to the ground. Its face pointing toward the backstreets of Santa Croce.

In the streets behind the cathedral, I am lost in a place I've never been. Some of the doors are as thin as chimneys. Some of the windows are bricked in. Some of the edges of some of the streets are lined with smooth old stones and my thin shoes slip, like I am running on a bed of feathers.

In the gutter of a roof a silver cat sleeps. In a window box a garden grows, the heads of the flowers catching the rain from the sheets that hang from a rope. Above the shoulders of some houses I see the gold domes of Florence and the fake *David*, and the cutout face of San Miniato, a toy city. Through the iron rails of a park gate children play, and it is late in the afternoon and now, in one of the windows, I see a girl with her two-flower bouquet. Me.

I hear someone laughing.

I turn.

His eyes are like river water. His hair is light. He wears one gold ring in his nose and a dark blue chip in his ear, and the sunflowers in his pink duffel bag have huge and curious heads.

It's you, I say.

I hold the flowers out to him—bruised and bent and breathless. I say, These are yours, or You dropped these, or maybe I say nothing, maybe I don't have the words, but he does.

An American girl, he says. His words right and his accent heavy. He crosses his arms, leans back. He studies me and I wonder what he sees. Dark hair. Pale hands. Two flowers. A girl who says nothing or maybe said something. A girl so far from home. He reaches across me, toward the flowers in my arms. He dials their faces toward the sky and leans back and smiles.

You should take care, he says. *Città di ladri.*

City of thieves.

Two lines in the wink of each eye. The start of a beard on his chin. He is taller than me, taller than Jack, a blond Italian.

You're always where I am, I say.

I've been watching, he says.

You—dropped these, I say. Lifting the flowers.

Left them, he says. *Per te.*

He smiles. Unzips the bag strapped across his chest. Sorts through the flowers he has stolen, one by one by one, choosing the fattest and dealing it to me, like this is a game of cards, or Hansel and Gretel, like this is what I followed him for—to take what he has taken.

Yours now, *si?*

A touch on my shoulder. A hand on my hand. *Real.* The zipper of his bag pulled shut again, careful, like someone protecting new eggs. He pushes off from the wall and a man on a bike with a basket goes by, three dogs in the basket, two yellow lemons. The bike creaks creaks creaks, and the boy stands there, his bootlaces loose on the stones.

You're an interesting girl, he says.

I've been watching, he says.

He touches the corner of his eye with a finger, like it's all in there, everything he's seen, everything I've done, everywhere I've been in Florence, everything I've stolen. He says, You took the corkscrew spring from the upholstery shop in the Oltarno. You took the kaleidoscope from the jeweler. You took the amethysts and the pillow. You took the hat and the tie and the stamps and the rubber pencil. You stole from Paperback Exchange.

You should be careful.

He fixes the bouquet in my arms and the bells in the cathedral ring.

I can't stay, he says. Someone is waiting.

But—

I'm Benedetto.

Na—dia.

He nods. Be careful, he says.

Of—

Everything.

He touches my hand. He twists the flowers in their bouquet of three and now he's running. The sound of his laces on the old, gray stones, the flowers in the duffel bag safe, protected.

In the window of the nearest shop stands a girl with pale hands and bright flowers.

I tell you this.

Tell me you see it.

21

And so the cat drags her in, Jack says.

He lies sprawled across the thin-cushioned couch, his bare feet hanging off one end and his ankles knobby. He lies there watching me, his Don't Be Hating on Me T-shirt tight from too many trips through the Laundromat soaker. He points the remote at the TV and snaps off the soap and the upstairs stilettos tap like fingers on a phone and all the plates in the sink are gone and the table is perfectly clean, no sign of anything, except for the rosemary sticking up in the mug and one bright tip of a neon feather.

No Mom. No Dad. No Perdita.

Were you kidnapped?

I shake my head.

Were you lost?

May—

You know what time it is?

Words bang in my head like meteorites. I see Mom and Dad and Jack and me outside in the night, long ago.

Eight o'clock, Nads. Eight o' Freaking Clock.

I step sideways, down the hall toward the twins' room. I keep the sunflowers close, behind my back. Jack pulls out his phone, punches two texts, waits for the phone to buzz back. Once. Twice. He looks up and I see, in the wide brow beneath his shag of hair, his crooked worry line.

You should try not to do this, he says. Try not to mess so much with Mom and Dad. Who are, by the way, out there looking for you.

I didn't mean—

Yeah?

I'm not trying—

Say it, Nads.

Like a needle lifting from a Maggie record, the song stops. I see the boy in the street. I feel the weight of the flower. I see break instead of color, and I can't find the next word. It's gone.

Yo, Jack says.

But I'm inside the borrowed room, locking the door. I'm lying down beneath the ship of stolen things. I'm holding the flowers that are hot as suns inside my broken hands.

The boy is real.

22

They're singing in the space between the backs of things, two of the restaurant boys and a girl in a green dress with a hat pinned to her head. Italian words to American songs. I hear Mom and Dad in my head as they sing—the long talk after they got back from searching the city for me. *You don't disappear like that. You don't go without telling us where you are. You know how much we worry, Nadia? How far we walked, looking for you? What are you doing? What are you thinking? We can get you help, sweetie. Dad knows a doctor.*

A doctor?

A neurologist.

Neur—o—logist.

I chopped the sunflowers from their stems, see? I pierced each thistling face at two opposite ends, pulled one silver chain through the east-end holes and one silver chain through the west-end holes so that the faces of the flowers are suspended and I have what I have—a three-story sunflower nest.

Which needs a ribbon—raw bright pink.

There are three faces of sun in a room lit by the moon. At the window I watch the waiters vanish one by one, until the songs are gone. *Neurologist.* In the great glass room where the bookbinder works nothing stirs. He has left his things within reach. The glue, the brush, the paints, the wall of wooden tools with their flat faces and their pointy ends, the heavy-handled scissors, the signatures, the threads, the ribbons streaming down from ceiling hooks, like the edge of a skirt, like feathers, like puppets from strings. It's all right there, and I am so freaking scared and my heart is pounding harder and harder, and suddenly I remember Mom last fall when it was just the two of us, out on the porch in West Philly, waiting on the neighborhood cat.

Mom and a bowl of milk on the porch.

Mom and a dish of crushed tuna.

Mom and a checkered blanket.

She'll come, Mom said. *She trusts us.*

Trust.

The cat came.

Trust is the word that keeps breaking.

There are birds nesting with thorns. There are birds stitching caterpillar silk. There are saliva nests and loom nests and milkweed nests and cattail nests and honeysuckle nests, nests loomed and folded and pounded and lined and feathered in and warmed, and there was the finch who saved herself and the chicks from the storm. Every nest is a miracle. It is something whole. A place to hide. A rescue.

Across the alley, the bookbinder sleeps. Bright ribbons hang from a hook above his window, and it's the dark start of another day.

Don't you dare, I hear you say. *Don't even think about it, Nadia.* But I remember the first steal ever, and how I could not help it.

My very first steal.

23

It was our last day in the city. We were leaving what we loved. The Victorian twin and the Schuylkill River moon and the stray cat with the broken whiskers that drank the milk Mom left her, and the birds, the blue birds in the locust trees, the red birds in the magnolias, the crows like black keys on the roofs of white houses, the finch and her chicks. We were leaving. It was hurricane weather. The planes were bad karma, grounded by clouds thick as steel plates. Mom and Dad and Jack and I were sitting in the airport rocking chairs looking out on the puddled tarmac and the gulls that couldn't break into the sky. We'd walked the terminals end to end—all of us, then me and Jack, then me alone.

My first steal was from the airport bookstore. My first steal was *Goodnight Moon*, the book my dad had read aloud when I was young, a lullaby song. The clerk was talking into her decal-sequined phone. The people passing by were rushing through. I took one book, a single one, slipped it into my carry-on. The clerk never noticed. No alarm was rung. I didn't run.

One thing stolen.

That night, high in the freezing sky, my parents slept across the aisle and Jack curled behind me and in the great green room there was a telephone and a red balloon and a picture of the cow jumping over the moon. And there were three little bears sitting on chairs and two kittens. It was so simple. I tore the pages from their bindings and the pages into strips, a muffled sandpaper sound. I worked the paper with the looms of my hands. The nest I built was the size of my palm. It was the calmest thing I'd ever seen.

Grapevine, oak twig, water reeds, snakeskin, rabbit fur. Straw, bark, lichen, milkweed fiber, fishing lines, milk crates, chimney hollows, riverbanks, holes, Easter grass. There are birds that sew. There are spit-building birds and mud architects and cream-colored birds that lay cream-colored nests into a scratch of cream-colored sand. High in that freezing sky everyone was asleep and Florence was coming and something was already wrong. A comb and a brush and a bowl full of mush and a quiet old lady . . . hush. The birds full of hush.

The skies were black and then they were bright, and this is how simple it was. Now, here, the sky is gallons of dark. It's a few hippo clouds and a million stars and a moon that is rounding the bend. There are no lights on in the back-alley places. The bookbinder sleeps. I just need one pink ribbon to finish this nest.

There's a steal coming.
It is not me.
It is all me.
You can't stop it.
Nobody can.

24

The sound of running feet.

The ruffling of Vitale ivy.

The stink inside the vestibule.

The cool air on Verrazzano.

Past the Laundromat, and through that one single alley that runs between and straight into the backs of things, I hurry. Across the patio where the waiters sing. Underneath the bulbed-light string. Toward the window where the bookbinder works. In the rubble I find a stone and toss it, a quick arrow. The glass shatters and echoes, and I have to work fast—reach for that one pink ribbon that hangs from its dark hook. Reach, and it's mine, and now I'm running again, between the backs of things, across the patio, beneath the lights, into the street, up Verrazzano, key in the lock.

Safe.

Almost.

There's a woman with stilettos just inside the door. She holds a small dog. She's smoking.

Buongiorno, she says.

Buongiorno.

I have been seen.

Me, the thief, who can hardly speak.

My heart is wild in my chest.

25

The water is hot cold thin. The bathroom light is ginger ale. The time is dawn. I stand in the shower until the water ends. Until it is only a trickle. Until my heart stops thundering and I can breathe again.

In the mirror above the sink, out of the cloud of shower steam, I see who I am—square jaw, shallow chin, nose rising at the tip, ears busting through the wet streaks of my hair. *You are the spitting image of your mom. You could be sisters,* is what everyone always says, but the girl in the circle of steam is me.

In the twins' room, in the Goldilocks drawers, I find jeans and a white tee, my nubby yellow sweater. I pull them on, stand in the window, look out onto the dawn. I watch the sun break and catch in the broken glass of the bookbinder's room, where the pink streak of ribbon is gone, and where he already is—the bookbinder with his bald head and his naked wrist, his shirtsleeves rolled to his elbows. He has a brush and a pan in his hands.

What is our plan? Maggie used to ask me. In her mother's kitchen, making eggs, she'd ask me. In her Simplicity apron—orange plaid with angel wings. With the pan sizzling, the butter melting, the eggs cracking, Maggie was asking, waiting, sliding a plate in front of me and wriggling her feet out of her open-toed clogs and sitting down across from me, and asking.

I always had the plan.

I fit my feet into my flats. I ponytail my hair. I open the door to the twins' room and lock it with the key. I walk very, very quiet under the ivy, past the buttons and winter coats and gallons of left-behind bleach, past spiceology and the blank face of the TV, past my dad's blank book. Through the tall windows of the front room of the Vitales' flat, I watch the neighbor's laundry drip and the bruised hour brighten. I will weave that pink ribbon into the sunflower nest. I hear somebody calling my name.

I open the window that opens to the street and lean.

You, I say.

Vieni con me.

26

He weaves through the early streets and the sky is breaking. He speeds, and I am holding on, my chest pressed to his leather back, his neon duffel bag like a folded wing. Through the alleys he weaves, past iron grates, over fat gray stones, toward the Lungarno, and now we are flying across the bridge, across the Arno. When the bridge ends, he slows, turns right then right again, onto a cement ramp that slopes straight down to the river, which is a bright blind spot, gold and pink. A concrete dam sits on the river's back like an archipelago.

There are people on the dam, fishing and drinking. There are two kids feeding mini dynamite sticks to the low river, and lovers, and he climbs off the Vespa and takes my hand. *Da questa parte,* he says. This way. We walk the back of this concrete whale past the fishermen, the drinkers, the kids scaring the fish with their explosives. We walk, and my feet slip on the green moss and he catches me and I slip again, and now I sit at his side, safe in the hands of a thief.

She saw me.

I left the bookbinder's window in smithereens.

We watch a slow boat row. We watch the nearby buildings burning with the low sun and the fisherpeople giving up on their catch, reeling in, smoking. We watch the river and the birds, the river and the birds, and the birds, the hanging branches, gutters, and coves, and the woman with the stilettos cannot find me.

Bello, he says.

The smell of coffee and bananas close. The scruff of a new beard close. The chip in his ear. He sits with his chin on his knees, his jacket short in the sleeves, the last inch of his jeans worn down to white threads, and time slides. The dynamite shatters the water and an egret hovers, and the smaller birds are like painted moles on the face of day. I see the valleys and hills of his toes beneath the leather of his boots. I see the gone places in the knees of his jeans and the hem of his T-shirt. Frayed. I see him, and this is not a dream. Benedetto.

Howdidyoufind me? I say.

I've been watching you, he says. Remember?

He lifts my hand and turns it over. He draws a finger across my palm. *Sei stata qui*, he says, touching a place at the base of my ring finger. You have been here. *E qui.* The joint of my thumb. And here. The place where my hand connects to my wrist. Also here. The highest part of my middle finger. Each touch of my palm a corner of the city. My hand the map that he draws. Verrazzano, he says, the tip of his second finger touching the tip of my fourth.

Città di ladri.

The boys with the dynamite send another stick into the low Arno and fish tails flap. Two lovers head down the concrete ramp and over the slick moss of the archipelago, and she slips, too, and he catches her, and they laugh. On the Ponte Vecchio, the jewelers have started to open their shops—clanging the windows and doors, and rattling the chains, and sending the seagulls into a squawk, and now an egret flies, its wings slicing the sky. When I lift my head and turn I see cars on the bridge behind us, rumbling and choking past.

Guarda, Benedetto says now. He unzips his duffel bag and digs in with his hand and retrieves a big petaled, freckled flower, dew on its tiger lily face, a small green caterpillar lying against its hairy stem.

Per te, he says.

I press the flower to my face and breathe. I feel the wet heat of tears, the blur of the day, and the egret flies again, overhead, and I look up and laugh.

Gli uccelli, he says.

Gli uccelli.

We sit and the river changes color and the Ponte Vecchio fills with tourists hunting for a jewel, a chain, a deal. Along the

Lungarno the walks grow crowded, and on the stem of the flower the caterpillar scrunches forward, and I say that once a long time ago, in the place where I really live, I found a finch in a fig tree. I say a storm blew in but the finch and her eggs stayed safe. I say this, or at least I try to say this, and it doesn't matter how we say what we say—neither of us fluent in English.

I like that story, he says.

I tell him that Philadelphia, where I come from, is a city of birds. I tell him everywhere you look there are feathers falling and there are nests made out of grass and rubber bands, spiderwebs and moss, the new branches of a fig tree, and in every single nest there's the hope of something new or saved.

He nods. He watches the river. The chip in his ear catches the sun.

Where did you go, I say. Yesterday?

I tell him with my hands, my heart. Somehow, he understands.

Why have you—been watching me?

Because you're interesting, he says.

Too interesting?

There's something you should see, he says.

27

Back on the Vespa, up the ramp, over the bridge, we ride the rough stones. Through the half streets, onto the sidewalks in the alleys, where the pieces of the street have been hauled out by jacks and machines. My arms around his waist. My cheek against his leather back. My heart like fumes. The birds above us fly in a crooked *V*, like we have them on a string. *Like someone had you on a string,* Dad said. The flowers are safe inside the duffel. The silk green of the caterpillar is safe on the long stem of the lily, and the woman with the stilettos cannot see me.

The roar and then nothing. The clutch and the key. Stop. We climb off and leave the Vespa by a rack of bikes and the crowd is against us—the thousands herding in from the train station across the way, their colossal suitcases like pets on a leash. One door takes us off the street and down some interior stairs into sudden quiet.

Chiostro Verde, Benedetto says.

We duck the turnstile, let ourselves in. It's like walking through a telescope toward a burst of solar, and I think, for one small moment, about the Vitales, the bookbinder's window, the latest steal. At the end of the corridor we turn into the broad, painted arcade that wraps the cloister green on all four sides. In the high parts of the arcade there are birds and wings, a story told in old paint. In the square of green beneath the open sky, cypress trees grow.

There is one fresco after another. There is sky and stone, the silence and calm, and Benedetto is telling a story about the paintings here. This man and his terrified dog. This wrenched tree. These broken barrels, tables, walls. These pictures from hundreds of years ago, barely holding on. *L'Arca di Noe*, Benedetto says. Noah's Ark. Painted by Paolo Uccello. A man named after birds.

He shows me the gray-grays and red-grays and blue-grays of the vanishing paintings. He shows me the strange world of broken things and corked perspective, birds and wings, and we are standing there together, and he leans against me and he takes my hand and there are bells ringing in the distance. He checks his watch. There's still time, he says.

He cuts away, toward the cloister's center. I follow him to the tallest cypress on the grassy green. He kneels, puts his fingers to his lips. In the shadow of the tree I kneel beside him and watch as he separates the branches of the tree, the branches like curtains, and now, in the dark shade, I see them—a pair of turtledoves, their breasts expanding with every beat of their hearts, their faces flicked sideways. The first bird is more anxious than the second. It spreads its wings and a few white feathers fall, drift to the ground. The second bird *turrs*, its neck going fat with every note it sings.

Per te, he says. I thought you would like it.

The birds hop the interior of the tree. They call to each other. They turr. Far, far away the church bells ring. The boy has to go.

Somebody needs me, he says.

28

Jack thunks Marcella down so hard that a bowl on the kitchen table jumps. Perdita looks up from under her pompodored hair. She wears big drippy sleeves and a short yellow skirt and ribbed tights, the same boots from yesterday, and in her hands she holds five swordfish steaks, one piled on top of the other. From her neck dangles that chain with its feather pendant—heavy and light, the tips of the feathers catching the steam that billows up from the oil in the skillet.

Nadia, Mom says, her footsteps coming quickly down the hall, a phone in her hand and lines in her forehead. Where the hell have you been? Sweetie. We've been worried.

Jack counts the mint leaves. Thirty-five. Perdita puts the garlic cloves into the heated oil. Jack reads Marcella slow and out loud, pretending nothing's wrong here, this is just life at the Caras', life with a mostly MIA sister. Mom asks me again: *Sweetheart.* She says Dad's out there, looking for me, and did we not already have a conversation, and could I not at least have left a note, and please, Nadia, answer. Jack chops chili peppers. He throws the thirty-five mint leaves into the pan. Perdita's necklace flies forward.

It's one o'clock, Mom says. She lifts her phone and calls Dad. Jack announces that mint is a cure for the common cold, mint is a cure for bad breath, mint is a cure for almost anything. Glares at me briefly.

Perdita watches him talk, watches me. She lifts one eyebrow and that's when I see the tiny little loop at the end of one brow, like a period at the end of a sentence, and now when she leans toward the pan again, to stir the mint, to watch the garlic glow and the saffron stir in, her chain clinks against the edge of the pot. She quickly shucks it off. Strings it across the back of a chair like a purse. Stands beside my brother. Gives his cheek a kiss.

Itookawalk, I say.

Don't do this, Mom says.

I'll go—find Dad.

Not a chance. You'll stay right here. Your father's coming home.

Pesce spada come la fa la rita, Jack says. Mom stands and walks across the room. Says something to Perdita, something to Jack, and now the door opens, and Dad's here, and Jack announces the spice of the day, which is really an herb, and I can't help it: Perdita's chain makes its way into my fist. A perfect fit. The hall at the

Vitales' is hurried with ivy. The closets are full of forgotten things. The twins' door unlocks and then it locks again. I pull the chain from the sleeve of my sweater.

What the hell, I think. What the friggin' hell?

If you cared about me, you would stop me.

29

The upstairs piano plays, but I don't know the song. The smell of lit cigarettes floats. Invisible fog. The song stops, and there is a parade of sharp-heeled shoes, and I wait, certain now that they are coming for me, but there is only silence up above, and Mom and Dad in the room next door, talking.

We can't wait.

We have to go.

Katherine's ready for us.

In the back the bookbinder works behind a wall of taped-up glass. Here, I work too, faster and faster—the freckled flower, the stolen chain, the tips of feathers, scissors and glue. The stalk bends and the bloom glows and everything is complicated, and I need the light of the moon.

Hey, someone says.

Is it you?

30

I wake to the sound of bricks being dropped to the ground, to glass things crashing. I wake in the bottom bunk, beneath the ship of steals. I listen for the sound of rain. No weather. I listen for the shoes above me, or a song. Nothing.

I lift the skirt of the twins' bunk bed and the nests are there—the old ones, the new one—tucked into the museum of my obsession, the beautiful and strange. I stand at the window and see the empty patio, the string of Christmas lights, and two men, like policemen, dusting the edge of broken things, and now I see the bookbinder himself, his bald head bright in the morning light, his glasses hanging from a chain around his neck. The police take notes on thin pads. They slip dust and shards into a plastic bag. They talk—a grumble of Italian—and I step back, very slow. I hear the sound of something coming. I open the door, lock it behind me, and the front room of the flat is like a storm blew through. A couch pillow hatting the head of the TV. The TV yanked away from the wall. The tubs and the buckets of ivy in the wrong places, pots and pans in a crooked stack near the sink.

Jack?

Can't find it, my brother says. Can't find it and told her I would.

A cord trails from the headphones at his neck. His hair is a mad porcupine. The dot on his chin is more like a beard. He shoves everything he touches—throws couch pillows onto the chair, chair pillows onto the floor, pots and pans into the sink. He's as close to tears as I have seen him since last year, when Dad came home and announced his sabbatical and Jack started listing everything he loved about Philadelphia, everything he would miss—Restaurant School's two-day-old muffins, that cat that came around, Wawa frozen cappuccinos, bluegrass at Fiume, the lights at Boat House Row, the chimney tower on Walnut Street, the man on Forty-Second who batons his cane and sings his Sammy Davis, Jr. tunes, the white house on Forty-Third that looks like it belongs at the beach. *We'll make it up to you,* Dad said. *We'll give you—*

You know what I'm talking about? You know that chain? Perdita's?

I stand, useless, helpless, in a gunked-up nightshirt, ruby-tipped fingers, the smell of glue. Chunky gold, green feathers, he says. Family heirloom stuff.

He twists the headphones around his neck and my fingertips are beating like ten out-of-kilter hearts.

Christ, he says, and then his phone buzzes and he pulls it from his pocket and reads the text. Two. Three times. He texts back, waits. Another message shivers in. He texts again. His shoulders sag. Exasperated. Worried.

Worst timing in the world, he says. Get dressed, he says. We're meeting Mom and Dad at the top of the hill.

What are you—talking about?

What do you think I'm talking about? Jesus. He tosses another pillow, pushes the couch with his foot, scratches his head.

Come on, he says.

Can't.

You have to.

I don't—want.

Jesus, Nads, do you think I want to go? Do you think I have time to babysit— And then he stops, like he's supposed to feel sorry for me, be über nice to me, and that hurts worst of all. My eyes are wet spots, burning.

All right, I say. I'm—

Just get changed, he says. Don't take so long.

31

Through the streets, with the schoolkids and the moms and the bikes and the bike bells and the nuns. Through the streets, my heart pounding. Jack is a shadow cast forward. He has the tuft of a lime-green feather riding high in his back pocket, the only evidence of Perdita's chain he could find, and every time he turns, I'm still here, walking behind him, and still he turns, like he can't trust me.

She thinks I took it, Jack says. Why would I do that? To Perdita? Shit.

My chest so tight.

At the Lungarno we cross to the riverside and walk west beneath the streetlamps. The sun is rising fast, splatting the horizontals of the bridges with a yellow pink. At the Ponte Vecchio the stacked boxes of the shops hang above the river. In the faces of the buildings along the Oltarno, the shutters are being pulled back, wood banging against wood and stucco and stone. I look for

Benedetto, for a Vespa, for dropped flowers, a sign, a way out of this, out of me.

Meet them on the hill. Tell them the truth. Tell someone.

The air is cool, the sun is warm. On the other side of the river, at the Michelangelo Piazzale, the fake *David* lies invisible behind a tail of fog. In the arcade along the Lungarno, two gypsies are kneeling side by side, their lips kissing the old stones, their lizard hands begging. A taxi out looking for a fare rides the street too close to the curb and Jack grabs my arms, yanks me safe.

What are you doing, he says. Christ.

Halfway across the Ponte Vecchio we stop at the lookout and stand side by side, looking east toward the start of the Arno, which is just a muddy creek, so far down from where we stand on this bridge that any catastrophe story seems like fiction, and I think of all the times I've said to Dad, *Prove it*. Prove your flood, as if anyone can prove anything, but Dad tries, shows me photographs of November '66, the bridges neck-high in the thick of river anger magnified. *The water ran twenty-eight feet high*, he said. *Higher. The bridge was like a dam*, he said, the capsized trees and cars and walls and windows of ruined houses pushing up against and through. Armchairs and jewelry boxes and portfolios and silverware and the split sides of sculptures and books all in the river by then. The river wanted nothing that it took. It dropped it, drowned it, pushed it, broke it, turned it into filth.

The river is a thief.

As am I.

The sun is blinking off. A fog is coming in. We leave the bridge and walk, feeling the fog's soft gray fur as we climb, its dampness seeping into our hair and skin. Jack half disappears out in front. I see his skater shoes and his frayed jeans hem, the bend of his knees, a hand, the lime-green feather, and the rest is gone, sucked into the thick mist, and when a Vespa passes, I turn.

Nothing.

We head up the long ramp of the road that rises along the massive stone wall of Fort Belvedere. There are places in the wall that have fallen. Patches where green, leafy things have settled in, as if someone has hung the ramparts with window boxes.

We don't talk. Sometimes a brother is a best friend, and sometimes a brother is a brother, and sometimes a secret is worse than a lie. There are olive trees on both sides of the road. Air the color of pearls and the sudden wild purple of flowers that erupt from vines tangled in the branches or caught in the thatched places of the wall. A girl with a bike appears at the top of the road and speeds toward us, a skateboard tied to her back. Jack turns and watches her fly. He stands there facing east and down, while I climb west and high.

Now Jack comes fast on the hard angle of asphalt behind me, passes me, makes his way up the hill and around the compass points and parapets of Belvedere, where the fog is breaking. They're not here, Jack says. Finds a stone. Kicks it.

Maybetheysaid—

Nine-thirty, they said. I talked to them. You didn't.

He kicks another chunk of rock. He looks back to where we came from, as if he will be able to see the missing chain and its tip of lime-green feathers from up here, a new perspective. When he takes a seat on the ribbon of grass beside the stone wall, I sit too— my feet flopped out, my foot turning around my ankle, my heart banging hard.

Tell me the truth, he says.

What?

Was it you? You who stole the chain?

I shake my head. He stares at me, now past me, and I try to stop the pounding in my chest—try to keep from standing, running, escaping, and now on the road, near the bend I see Mom and Dad on the rise, a woman between them, her silver hair fluffed at the ends like a cashmere hem.

Jack stands and stuffs the feather deeper into his back pocket. I hide the weave my fingers have started to make with the grass that grows tall by the wall. Dad stops on the road, out of breath, and then Mom does, and the woman does, and her gaze is cool. She shakes Jack's hand. She takes mine. She looks into my eyes.

This is Katherine, Dad says. A friend.

Ciao, she says, but she's American—dusty Doc Martens on her feet, a yellow cotton blouse that lets the muscles on her arms show through, and a pair of khaki trousers with scatter lines above the knee where the hanger was.

Good day for a view, Dad says.

A beautiful day, Mom says. Her eyes going from me to Jack to me like she can't believe I'm actually here, like Jack just pulled off some giant magic trick, and now we're walking—Mom and Dad and Katherine ahead, and Jack beside me on the incline, his shadow cutting the sun on my face.

Who? I ask.

Jack shrugs. He kicks another stone down the hill and watches it fall. He stuffs his hand into his back pocket, fingers the feather, and he climbs, and we climb until we reach the highest bend, the open door, the ticket lady, from whom Dad buys five passes, breathless.

Fort Belvedere is a Medici villa inside fortress walls, four-hundred-something years old. That's what Dad says. It's a museum for modern sculpture—the busts of naked women, a pinwheel of bronze in the sun. Look at us, Dad says. Here we are. Dad talks prof talk about the guy who designed this place for the rich Grand Duke. He says how many old walls are missing now, how the star-shaped fortress was mostly cut down to make room for the city's growth. He points to a tunnel we can't see—the secret passages between Belvedere and the Pitti Palace and Florence proper over the bridge. He says the word again—*secrets*—then *fireworks* and *theater*, but his words are snipping into static. I head toward the cliff, the tumbled garden, the view. I stand there, leaning north, watching Florence click on and off, looking for the boy, Benedetto, who can draw my story on my hand, who will listen.

On a Vespa. With a duffel. He is out there, looking for me.

Lean. You'll see.

Reach.

Hey, I hear a shout, feel a hand on my shoulder.

Whoa, Nads. It's Jack, behind me, Dad, too, Mom running from wherever she was, her black hair cinnamon in the sun. You were kinda tipping there.

Sweetie, Dad says. Honey. Didn't you see?

I feel Katherine's hand on mine, her cool fingers, her words. I hear her saying that it's a gorge, that there are rocks beneath those flowers, that it's steeper than I think; a woman died. Her one hand on my shoulder and her other hand on my hand, and she's walking me backward, her voice calm, and Dad is telling Jack to give me some room. Mom slips her hand into Dad's, holds it tight. White knuckles.

I told her to stop, Jack says, to Dad, and Dad says, I know you did. She's fine. She's here.

Katherine finds a bench and we sit, her beside me. I lean back, and she's there, her arms strong inside their yellow sleeves. Count with me, Nadia, Katherine says. Breathe. She starts and I let her count all the numbers backward. Ninety-seven, ninety-six, ninety-five. I let her start and finally I count, too, seventy-three, seventy-two, and Dad's face comes in close like a missing-pieces puzzle, his eyebrows tangled up in his lashes. I close my eyes and I can hear Maggie.

I'm right here, she says.

You're okay.

32

The room is square and polished bright. There are red tiles on the floor and there is music above my head and painted stucco. Two open windows and a wall of glass jars on glass shelves. There's a girl on a bed beneath a sheet, and she is me. There's gauze on my left hand, like a glove, a little spot of blood in the white gauze, prick of ruby.

Here you are.

Her fingers on my wrist, counting the pulse. Her cashmere hair floating. Shhh, she says, and I sit up, startled. Nowhere to be, she says. We have time.

There's a lemon wedge in a glass of seltzer. She gives it to me and tells me to drink—all of it, slow, champagne bubbles in my nose. She asks me how long it's been since I have slept, since I've had a proper meal, and I ask her who she is.

My name is Katherine, she says, but I meant what am I doing here, where's Mom, where's Dad? Everybody's in the room next door, she says. You've had a little spell.

Where are—

We're home, she says. My home. Finish it, she tells me, about the drink. Or maybe the sentence.

She cuffs my arm, pumps me up, looks down, makes notes. She pokes a thermometer into my ear, puts her two fingers on my wrist again and glances away, to count. She has a clipboard and a purple pen. The noise of the pen on the paper like a window being squeaked.

All of it, she insists, gently. You're dehydrated.

I'm okay.

All of it, she repeats. She takes the glass when I'm done, puts it on the shelf behind her, turns back to me, clink. Two big pots of ferns on the floor. A miniature *David* on the windowsill.

Can we talk a little? she says.

I'm really—

Can you tell me why you're so tired?

I never—sleep.

Hmmmm, she says. Never?

Not really. Not—

She writes something down. Raises her eyes. Writes again. She waits for me to say more, but that's it: *Not really.* You came close out there, she says. Too close to the edge.

I'm—sorry.

She lets the pen dangle from its clipboard string. She takes a seat on a simple wooden stool that I didn't see until now. In this room, she says, there are no apologies. Ever. You came close to the edge, and we worried. You're tired, and we want to help you. You hurt your hand. No blame here. No anger. Tell me what you mean by never.

Every word is clear. The room is peaceful, like the cloister was peaceful, like being with Benedetto was peaceful. Benedetto. I straighten, stare out the window, look for him.

I can't rem—ember.

What can't you remember?

The last time I really—slept.

Let's start with last night. Tell me how it was.

I try to tick the hours back in my head; I can't. I see two turtle-doves and a boy on a Vespa. A bright moon. A new nest. Maggie's red hair. Jack at the Vitales'. Mad.

The Vitales arestillthere, I say. Intheapartment. They left them-selves be—hind.

Who are the Vitales?

It's their flat. They belong. Where we are.

And this makes it hard to sleep? She hasn't moved. The hem of her hair brushing her shoulders.

I curl into a question mark, try to think. The paper crinkles. A doctor's bed. She waits.

You're my father's—friend?

Your father called me, yes.

And you knew the woman who—died? The one who—fell from the ledgeatBelvedere?

They brought her to me, she says, that's all she says, and I don't want to imagine, but I do—a woman on a ledge walking above Florence, a woman falling, a cracked woman on this bed. Katherine sits on the stool and waits, and finally she tells me to rest for now, that we'll talk later. Still she doesn't move, stays where she is, her eyes on me, pale and blue, gray at the rims. She touches my gauze-gloved hand with her cool fingers, and I close my eyes.

The egret's talking, I say now. Do you—hear it?

Yes, she says. I do.

The birds are—everywhere, I say. The birds. Their nests.

She listens. There are more birds, different birds drawing the long notes out of their feathery breasts, then cutting the songs into quick chit-chits.

Do you like them? she asks. The birds?

I nod.

And you've always loved birds?

More and more—lately.

Hmmmm, she says. I like them, too. So determined to sing. So fearless. She turns slightly, her ear toward the window now. Can you tell me about your hand?

My hand.

I've cleaned it up, it should be fine, but if you could tell me . . .

I couldn't—help it.

You had a braid of some sort in your hand. A braid of tall grass. Elaborate. Intricate. Do you remember?

I shake my head.

I've saved it for you. In an envelope. Remind me, she says. Before you leave. So unusual. Beautiful, really. I don't know how you did that, with three long blades of grass.

It just hap—pens.

Tell me more.

Sometimes.

Hmmmm, she says. She writes something down, and then looks at me, lays the back of her hand across my forehead, pulls the hair away from my face. She picks up her pen and writes again.

You're having trouble with words, honey. Aren't you?

They're just—

Slow?

I nod. Slow.

In there, but slow?

Not all the time. Not always—there.

Hmmm, she says. Do you know when this began?

Inthespring? Something like—the spring? Or maybe? I don't know. I can—think, I say. I just can't—

Speak, she says.

I nod.

Hmmm, she says. Writes something down.

I can't be—crazy, I say. I can't be. Jack says—

I said nothing about crazy.

I didn't mean to get so—close to the—I just wanted to—

You know what I said, Nadia.

No apolo—gies?

That's right. No apologies. Everything we say to each other is just what we say to each other. No accusations. No crimes. Nothing to be embarrassed about. That's the rule here. That's what we'll live by.

She stands and pulls the stool across the red tile to a place beneath the window. She turns for a moment to watch the sky. I close my eyes and see me high above—a girl on a bed in a room. I see the broken star of the Belvedere wall, the city blinking on and off, the boy out there on his Vespa, Uccello's birds, cloister silence, a gold chain, my father, my mother, Jack. Katherine walks back across the room, her boots on the floor.

No one's mad at you, Nadia.

I feel her hands pulling my hair to one side, her fingers on my pulse. I feel her waiting, but I've said all I can, my own thoughts coming to me like a dream.

You'll tell me more when you can, she says. Okay?

I say okay.

Here, she says. I open my eyes and see her reaching up to a glass shelf to retrieve a tiny clay bell with a weathervane top. If you need me. She lays it down beside me, on the crinkle paper on the bed.

Katherine?

Yes?

How do you . . . My dad?

That's a story for someday.

You're American, I say. But you—

That happens all the time, she says. People fall in love with Florence. Get some rest, she tells me. I'll be next door if you need me.

Time is a white cloud.

Time is drifting.

33

The room is dim. The glass jars on the glass shelves are still and the windows are open and somewhere, closer now, there is the sound of silverware, the smell of carbonara, voices.

I close my eyes and I see Maggie and me in West Philadelphia—someone playing bluegrass and a big fan above our heads motoring the warm air through. *Listen,* Maggie said, and was it summer, do you know, when my best friend was so small and so strong and so lit up inside with all that noise and bluegrass, and when no one knew that something was wrong with me? No one would have guessed it.

I see you're awake.

It's Dad in the room on the stool across the way. The window behind him is closed, its panes like a mirror. There are shadows beneath Dad's eyes, the back of his head reflected in the window, all those glass jars on glass shelves, the birds quiet.

What time is it?

Dad pulls up his sleeve, checks his watch. Just past six.

The whole day's gone.

You slept, Nadia. You were peaceful. How are you?

I'm—

I try to sit, but I feel dizzy. I try again and now Dad's at my side, his big hands steadying me, helping me, slowly. Like I don't have any bones. Like I'm all melt. Steady.

You must be hungry, Dad says.

I don't—

Can you stand up? Katherine's been cooking.

I say I'm okay, but the room wobbles. Dad helps me up from the crinkle bed, stands with me until my bare feet are steady on the floor. He slips his arm around me and guides me across the tiles through a door I hadn't seen, into a large square room, where Katherine sits at a table built for two in a room of white, some gray stones rubbing through the thick walls. Along the wall, carved out of granite, is a sink, a half refrigerator, an old stove. There are three light-wood cabinets hanging above, and through each of the handles is looped an embroidered dish towel—purple, yellow, pink.

You've had us worried, Dad says, pulling a chair out for me to sit on, moving the books on the chair to the floor, never taking one arm from me, being sure. He says that Mom and Jack had to leave earlier, that we'll just have some dinner, that Katherine's been cooking, that we're working toward a plan.

You need time with someone who might understand what's going on, Dad says. Someone who can watch you, talk to you. Your mother and I . . . we don't have answers. Your mother and I . . . we just . . . Nadia . . . we love you. You know that we do. Katherine is a neurologist. Retired now, but famous. She knows doctors. She can help you.

Katherine serves the carbonara from a single pot as Dad talks. She takes flecks of parsley from a Pyrex dish and sprinkles them on top.

Still warm, she says. Sitting down and letting me take it in, waiting for me to ask questions, maybe, but I have none. I don't understand, but I do. Katherine is a neurologist. We need answers.

Dad gets up to crank the windows closed. There is a stack of books on the floor, a floral couch, a table of more books—Italian, American—newspapers, a small TV that looks like the first TV ever built. On the windowsill sits a miniature of the *biblioteca* that we pass each day on our way through Santa Croce, and beside that, tipping toward the glass, is a portrait of Michelangelo—small as a postcard, gold-framed.

More? she asks me.

It's good, I say.

She gets up, fills my plate, rinses a bunch of grapes, and fits them into a tall white bowl—round as miniature Christmas balls and bright as garnets. She carries the bowl and the plate to the table and slips into her seat, and I see how tall Katherine is, even sitting. They talk without me. They talk the day, and they talk gardens, carbonara, fortress walls, olive trees, tourists, the never-ending restoration of the Uffizi, and every now and then they steal a glance at me, to see, I guess, how I am settling in, to not force too much against me. I let my thoughts go—to the Green Cloister, the pair of birds, the painted stories in red and gray, Benedetto, nests, the ship of steals, Perdita's chain; yes, Jack, I stole it.

They are remembering the flood. They are remembering all that was ruined and piled into trucks and taken to tobacco barns and textile plants and heated up, dried out. They are talking weights and smells and all the people who came to Florence to help. Mud Angels, she calls them. The saviors of the flood.

The city's worst moment, she says.

The city's best moment, he says.

Yes. And they look at me.

How are you? Dad asks me.

I've taken your whole— I start. I'm— I can't finish.

Katherine lifts her hand. You don't have to talk, she says. Just relax, if you can. We'll talk later. Start tomorrow. Get at the heart of this. We can do that, Nadia. We're on the same team.

She crosses her arms at her chest and leans back into the dim light of the white room. I hear a car on the street outside, a quick rumble of laughter. I listen for the boy.

I suppose it's getting late, Dad says.

Too late to walk all that way now, Katherine says.

She fiddles in her pocket and finds her phone. She dials quickly and speaks Italian. She offers me a cookie, and I take it, watching her, watching Dad. It takes a while before the taxi rumbles up the hill, but when it does, Dad stands first and helps me with my chair. He puts his arm around me.

Tomorrow, Katherine says. We'll start fresh.

She finds the envelope with the braid of grass. Gives it to me. Says, It's really something. What you have done with grass.

It's just—

The taxi is here. The door is open. Dad is helping me into the backseat that smells like licorice and ham. The taxi slings to the ground, like it's missing some parts. The door slams and the driver U's, and we take the hill down. The lights of Florence are twinkling on. Lamplight is reflected in the Arno. A group of students grows rowdy in the street; a boy plays an accordion to a hotel window. We're back to the Vitales', where everything is missing, and where I cannot hide anymore.

Jack is out.

Mom is asleep.

I need to know who—Katherine is, I say.

A friend, Dad says. You can trust her.

34

She was nineteen, Dad says. I was twenty.

He presses his hands into a temple beneath his chin. Pours wine into a water glass, goes to the window and stands and watches because a new storm is rolling in, rain is streaking the windows, and Jack is out there somewhere. Every time Dad checks his phone, every time he texts Jack, nothing happens, the phone stays silent, and I know that Jack is out there begging for mercy but I say nothing. I have asked Dad to tell me Katherine's story.

Dad puts his big hand into his white hair. He checks the phone again, puts it in his pocket. He says, Katherine Goldrath, and then he says, Mud Angels. He says there were hundreds like her who came to Florence after the flood. November 4, 1966. The Arno had spoken.

But rivers don't—

They do, he says. Rivers, he says, are always speaking.

Katherine was a sophomore at Penn, Dad says. I was a junior. We were taking the same class with Frederick Hartt, the leading authority on Renaissance art, the bon vivant. When news of the flood broke—when it was the front page of every newspaper, the ruinous flood, the death of art, the loss of culture—Hartt left for Florence at once, to help plan some kind of rescue. Katherine left school one week later. What was the point, she said, of knowing anything about the past when a city was in need right now. When arms and legs and hands could help. Lifting and sorting and drying.

She left to—help.

Katherine knows how to help, Dad says. You can trust her.

I need to know that I can trust her.

Tell—me.

She was driven from the airport in the back of a truck to the brown outer slick of the city. The river had sucked itself dry, left its dark teeth everywhere, according to Katherine in the letters she wrote and sent. The city stunk of the rotted flesh of capsized fish, the bloated loaves of floated bread, the sewage that had risen out of its medieval pipes and slithered into houses, curtains, pots. It burned to breathe. The stench went to her throat—the toxic *nafta*, the devil's incense.

There were mounds of martyred cars, brown lakes, empty places where the old stone streets had been. She wrote more letters: *You should come. We need you.* She was an American woman among the many who had come—from Fiesole, Siena, Roma, Milan, Sweden, Paris, Scotland, West Berlin. Some of them carrying transistor radios and letting the Beach Boys sing.

She was . . . Dad stops. She was . . . And now he stands at the window, thinking, and I sit here waiting for the rest of this story about this girl who was once just a little older than me and chose a city of ruin and made ruin the place that she lived. I wait and Dad says nothing, watching for Jack, until he turns around and continues.

There was a boy Katherine's age with a beard who had rafted in from the country on the back of an old road sign, Dad says. Sixty kilometers, he told her. No other way in. There were four Italian Boy Scouts who had wedged a piano onto the street and were playing duets for the sweepers. There were Red Cross stations and rusted machines, poor pumps, heaps of buttons, the springs of mattresses. There were unrescued people up on their roofs, a baby born beneath stars, children lowering *damigiana* from their windows, calling, *Bread. Fresh water. Warm milk. Take what we have.*

She slept one night on a thin mat on the cold stones of the Palazzo Pucci.

She slept in the back room of a flooded store, the birds still dead in their cages.

She slept among nuns in a monastery, fitting her stiff boots and black bandanna onto the rack above her head.

She slept in a rubber boat with two other girls her age—Danish girls.

She made do. They all did.

Dad circles through the room, pulls at his ear. He walks in and out of the shadows and returns to where he was, by the window. Watching the streets for Jack. Watching the shadows.

Dad?

But he's gone quiet again. He's standing there watching the one light in the flat across the street that never turns itself off when it rains. I close my eyes to listen to the streaming rain, and I think of Katherine, her fossil tracks in the mud, the blue and red flames burning in a city sick with cold, the letters she wrote home to Dad, and I wonder why anyone would hope, how anyone could. There is someone out on Verrazzano, drunk and singing football songs, and Dad strains to see if it's Jack. He lifts the cuff of his shirt to check the time, and I stand up beside him now, look out on the street, and the song is gone and the street is empty—no Jack, no Benedetto, if there was ever a boy named Benedetto.

Outside the sound of rain is sliding from rooftops. Inside it's Dad and me in the room and in the window glass, blurry, and now he pours himself another glass of wine and stands looking out into the street and I stand beside him and he says, I'm sorry I dragged you here to Florence, Nadia. You were so much happier at home. I've been selfish.

Dad, I say.

Dad.

It's not your—fault.

You kids, he says. Making me old.

You're not—

I've always been old. Your mom and you and Jack: you're the closest thing to young I have.

He puts his arm across my shoulder, pulls me to him. His rumpled shirt, his worried heart, my tears flooding the cotton of his shirt. I'm afraid, too, he says after a long time. But we're in this together, sweetie. All of us. The Caras and Katherine.

We stand, the story undone. We stand without talking, stand watching Verrazzano through the front window of the Vitales' flat until finally, down the street, we see a pair of Lunar Springs running: Jack. He hurries through the rain, his hoodie up, his bright shoes splashing the puddles. The door below us opens and shuts, and the shoes squeak in the stairwell, and the key fits into the lock. Jack throws his hood back, kicks off his shoes, rubs the rain out of his hair, looks up and sees us.

Yo, he says.

Dad reaches his arm out toward him, and now Mom comes, sleepy, down the hall, and we stand in the circle of us.

35

In the bathroom I strip off my clothes and stand in the hot shower until the pressure falls away and the water trickles to a slow circle at my feet and I step out. In the fog of the bathroom mirror I see myself tipping over the ledge into the city. I see myself on the back of a Vespa. I see myself on the dam of the river. I see myself kneeling beside the boy to watch two turtledoves singing. I see myself breaking things, weaving things, losing things, crazy. I see myself, and I am too many people.

The air grows cold. I dig the key out of the pocket of the jeans I've thrown to the floor and unlock the door to the borrowed room and everything I fear is true.

Someone's left her life behind.

And now, all of a sudden, I remember Maggie and me in Second Mile Style—weaving up and down the crooked aisles. We sit in the La-Z-Boys. We shake the button jars, like a pair of maracas.

We put the plastic dolls in the floppy hats and then we pose them on the rocking chairs, and now Maggie finds a pair of ice skates with a sniff of winter in them, but this isn't what she came for. She came for the buckets in the aisle over, stacked upside down like party hats, the colors of Crayola. There's a dozen of them and she wants them all—takes each one and holds it up to the window light so that it catches the sun, the fake glitter inside the old plastic, the little bits of sand that got caught in the handle or the rim.

This, she says. *Here*.

Her hair in a ponytail. Her face brighter than her hair. Beads on the fringe of her faux-leather skirt. She spins. The beads chatter.

We carry the buckets back to her house, three on each of our four arms, like bracelets, and some of the kids from the stoops ask what's going on, but Maggie won't say. *You'll see*, she says.

Her parents are gone. She puts some Carly Simon on. She covers the braided rug between the beds with old newspaper, then stacks each bucket one by one by one in a line across the old news. She tells me to stay where I am, and I do—stand by her window watching the skies of West Philadelphia, the birds of West Philadelphia—the peregrines and red-tails and finches and crows flying by and looking down and seeing me and I hear Maggie on the stairs and Maggie down the hall, breathing heavy and walking slow, calling, *Close your eyes*.

I close my eyes.

Okay, she says. *Ready.*

It's a cardboard box and it's full. She bends down and slips it onto the floor—careful, slow—and inside the crepe paper faces of living poppies glow: orange and lemon and red and purple and white and pink. They have huge heads and their stems are so thin and some of them are still too shy to bloom.

Happy birthday, she says.

She goes back downstairs, to her dungeon basement, and comes back up again, a bag of dark-chocolate soil in her arms. She goes down one more time and this time she has two of her garden shovels in her hands, and two pairs of gardening gloves and two aprons, everything for both of us.

We'll plant them first, she says.

We pour the soil into the buckets. We sing to Carly Simon. She puts another record on. Outside the kids are playing in the streets and the Saturday ice cream truck is singing its song several blocks off and the birds are up there in the sky and it takes a long time to fill the buckets just right and to plant the poppies just right along the edges of the buckets, out of the way of the handles. When we're done Maggie has dirt under one eye.

She takes off her gloves.

Takes off her apron.

Check this out, she says.

She pushes the window up high. We line the buckets up on the floor nearby—careful not to spill, careful with the fragile

heads of the poppies, and now she's careful as she climbs, through the window, toward the sky, into the arms of the locust outside.

I need a bucket, she says.

Wait till you see.

You're completely crazy, I say. Like crazy is the funniest word in the world, crazy is other people.

I lift the purple bucket with the yellow poppies off the floor. I hand it to her through the window. She loops its handle over a nearby branch and she laughs like Maggie does.

Bucket number two, she says. *If you please.*

She hangs a blue bucket with red poppies. She hangs a green bucket with orange poppies. She hangs a white bucket with purple poppies. She hangs a red bucket with white poppies and every time she does it takes longer and longer as she works the branches and the twigs farther away on the tree. There is a crowd of kids below her. The mailman has stopped on his route. Two cats are in the across-the-street windows watching her every move. When she's finally finished hanging the very last bucket—when the tree is lit up with poppies and buckets and the glitter of the sun, when there's a crowd out there, and Mrs. Ercolani is home—Maggie stands, tall and completely triumphant.

World's greatest miracle, she says.

World's best friend, I say, and I sleep a long ti~~me~~
name rising throu~~gh~~

36

My cheek against his leather. My arms around his waist. Florence a chessboard. We go north and south, avoiding the start of the crowds, the early businessmen, the shopkeepers, the nuns. We go east, where the tourists aren't and the air smells like the chill inside unpopular churches, the abandoned storefronts. We cross the Arno and fly toward the Pitti Palace, and I hold on in this strange and early morning.

At the far edge of the city, Benedetto stops in the shade of triangle trees, swings his duffel bag across one shoulder, and takes my hand. Across the low part of a fence he leaps, then reaches his long arms for me.

We walk a pebble path, between trees, don't stop at the signs. There are hedges now, and marble grotesques and a pond and an island at the center of the pond, and Perseus on a white marble
limbs of old tree branches lace together, into

The running trickle of thin blue water. The dark squirrels scattering leaves. We step off the thin path and into the deep woods, and nobody is here but us—Benedetto and me, in the middle of a darkening morning.

On a bench deep in the woods, we sit—his legs too long for his hips. A crucifix hangs from a chain link at his neck, and when he pulls me close, I smell Vespa, leather, seeds—real things. He whistles—a real song, one fluttering tune, like helium streaking through the lips of a balloon. A long note. Three snips.

Look, he says. I follow the direction of his finger until I finally see them—a family of green woodpeckers beneath the trees, their long beaks and sticky tongues drilling the earth, their bodies the color of dried grass, their heads red as Maggie's hair. Hammering and twisting, yaffling.

Per te, he says.

We watch the birds in their clown heads, their green suits. We listen to them talk, the birds of Florence. The sky is so high above the leafy shield that we are cloistered in, but the storm is definitely coming. The birds know. They watch the boy and me, nervous. They crackle in the underbrush. They look up sideways and there's a crack of thunder overhead, and the rain falls but not hard, not yet. Benedetto bends over to the bag at his feet. Unzips. Pulls a yellow rose from the neon pink, its bud still tight and new.

He has a Michelangelo face. He starts to talk and I listen. About the cats in Florence and the monks at night. About the view of the city from the Duomo. About leather, something about leather, a shop in the bottom of the cathedral. Which cathedral? Santa Croce. Where? Past the Dante. Through dungeon doors. A man named Carlos. A leather workshop in a cathedral? *Si.* He says he never knew his father. He says his mother is a survivor. He says, You know about the flood? and I say, I know something about the flood, and he smiles.

Then you know me, he says. You know my history. You know my mother.

He tells me how it was, the stories his mother told him, which are the stories her mother told her, years ago. *Alluvione di Firenze.* Water rising from the river, rising from the basements and sewers, lifting the cars off the street, breaking the bridges in two, running up the ladders and the stairs, everything floating. He tells me about the men up to their waists in the water and the jewelry boxes they wore on their heads, the books they carried in their arms, the paintings on their shoulders, the bowls full of knives and spoons in their hands, the rescued puppies. He tells me like he was there, but he wasn't there. This is his city's story, his mother's story.

She was, he says now, a baby in the flood. She was, he says, floating in *how you say?* In a—

He describes the shape with his hand—not a coffin, but a box, not a square box, a rectangular box, a box with flowers.

Window box?

Si.

A baby floating in a window box. His mother, the survivor.

He talks—accidents, luck. He says—the tourists can't understand. He wants—something, again, about his mother. The rain is falling in its own rain country. Benedetto is building his words with his hands, wanting me to understand, and now, sometimes, into his stories I slide my stories. Maggie. Philadelphia. The cat and the bowl. The garden after the storm. The finch who survived the storm. Maggie's birthday present. Nests. I don't know what he understands or how well I say it. I don't know how much time is passing. I don't know what I'm leaving out, yet somehow, with Benedetto, it doesn't matter.

He lifts my hand like he did on the dam. He traces the blisters and splinters beneath the gauzy glove that Katherine wrapped on. Thunder cracks overhead and the rain slips through the canopy—small and cold in the part of my hair; beads, like pearls, on his collar.

What did you do to yourself? he asks.

I shake my head.

Tell me, he says. Touching the fraying gauze with the back of his thumb. Working a loose splinter free. Pulling a scab of glue from a fingertip. Showing it to me. He leans in for the truth, but words are so hard now, the stories I want to tell.

Trust me.

I do.

Tell me.

Siamo la stessa cosa, he says, but we're not the same thing, and the rain falls harder, and it is time to find my way to the top of the hill, to neurology, to answers. I have to get there before I disappear completely, before there is no hope at all, before I lose my way forever in this city.

I want to tell the boy that the girl I was could have fallen in love with the boy he is. I want to tell him in one long complete unbroken sentence. He takes my hand before I do and turns it in his. He puts one arm across my shoulder and we sit there and the church bells ring in the distance.

Something's very—wrong, I say.

There are freckles on the ridge of his nose. There is a damp curl through his hair. We're all running from something, he says, or I think he says it, and he lifts his hand to my chin and brushes the tears from my eyes and comes toward me, very close, and I feel his lashes brush up against my skin.

I'll be here, he says. If you need me.

His lips on mine are fog and birdsong. They are the smell of leather and the raw, quickening rain. He holds my head with the palm of his hand—all that is broken and hurting.

Don't forget this, he says.

Don't forget me.

After a long, long time he divides the curtain of trees with his hand. He stands up, he helps me. The rain falls from signs, it falls from the ledges of my cheeks; it is forever falling.

37

Her white dress floats to her anklebones. The couch is green; its legs are swans. Her glasses hang from a beaded chain at her neck, and now she shuts the door behind me and turns off the sound of the rain, and says, Thank you, Nadia, for coming.

She leaves and comes back. The rain slides down the windows, past the Michelangelos, the three clay teapots, the china cats, and it is cold. I close my eyes. When I open them she is toweling the storm out of my hair.

Let's get you into some warm clothes, she says.

I trade my shirt for one of hers, my sweater for another, my jeans for a skirt. I think of the hills I've climbed and the boy I've left behind, and the circle of Caras, and she brings me tea. Tells me it's a little past noon. She has called my dad. I can stay as long as I'd like—no, actually, you will stay, Nadia. I lower my face toward the steam of the tea. I let the tea burn my tongue.

You're still shivering, she says. She walks away and comes back, brings me a quilt from another room—red with gold threads.

Ancient. She pours me another cup of tea and now she fills a blue mug of her own, and she sits in the striped chair, a big fluffy chair, watching me, waiting.

One of the twins—left her story behind, I say at last, and she looks up and asks if this is still a worry.

To leave a story behind, I say. Toloseone.

What if the story is there when the girl returns? she says.

What if she doesn't?

What?

Return?

This worries you.

Yes. Very much. IamafraidIwon'treturn.

The tea is dark orange. A lemon seed floats. Another burst of rain hits the windowpanes, and the glass looks flooded and cracked and a caterpillar of white fog rises. Everything else is still. Everything else is silent. Storm and smoke.

Getting close to one o'clock, she says. And every tick of time is less of me.

38

When I wake I'm on the old couch and the clouds through the windows are low and Katherine is in the kitchen, turning a spoon in a pan. Onions. Bay leaves. Garlic. Rosemary. Tock on the wall. A little past two, she says.

She's wearing jeans now, an orange shirt open at the neck. She leaves the spoon in the pan and crosses the room and presses her wrist against my forehead—the blue beat of a vein. The rain has stopped. There is sun through the streaks on the panes. The face of a glass apple on the sill. Katherine carries a tray from the kitchen, two plates, and we sit side by side on the worn couch, and she says we should eat, or we can eat, if I want to, do I want to?

You were sleeping, she says.

She says the sky is set for a good bruising—so much storm, so much sudden sun. She says the days are often long on the hill, and that she's glad I came, that lunch alone is never as good as lunch with a new friend. My husband's specialty, she says, about the dish she's made. He was a fan of bay leaves, she says. Bay laurel. An herb that takes its time coming into its own.

I wonder if her husband is here, near.

She says he's been gone a long time.

I wonder if he was American. She says he was Italian, short and very wide. A perfect man. He sang, she says. He cooked. Sometimes I talk to him, still.

She stands, crosses the room. She reaches a planked table with a single drawer and chooses a photograph in a silver frame. She sits beside me on the couch so that I can see what her husband looked like years ago. Irresistible, she says.

She has a long neck, a few freckles on her chest, a mole on one side. She has two gold posts in her ears, like the first earrings ever, like she's never thought to buy another pair. She studies the picture and then she stands again, sets it back down into the dust ridges it came from and begins to dig through the pile of things on the floor. A mountain of books, a landslide. Some of the books are falling, and some are sliding, and there are magazines in there, illustrations, an envelope of paper clips that spill, and at last she finds what she was looking for, a book of photographs, and I wonder, is this it, the start of the cure? Nothing but us and slow time.

Your father, she is saying, is another lovely man. The smartest man I ever met. She sits by my feet on the floor.

Her book of pictures has wood covers. The pages between are gray-black, thick as construction paper, everything bound together with a leather cord, and when she turns the pages now some of the pictures fall out—square photographs, bleached colors, words written onto their backs. Words and years, lines and loops, ink like spiderwebs. There are girls in minis and boys in peace beads, thin ties, long hair, blue jeans, wide belts with brass buckles, and there is a girl holding two miniature turtles on the palm of her hand, and in this picture ten girls have made a kneeling pyramid. Four. Three. Two. One. The top girl is off balance, laughing. That was me, Katherine says. Ruining the pyramid. I squint. The almost-falling girl is a thin, beautiful girl and her hair is a black fountain and she wears a turtleneck tunic, a pair of climbing boots, two gold posts in her ears.

That was—you?

Me, she says. They shouldn't have trusted me at the top.

She has stories for most of the photographs. She takes her time. She says, We were young back then. She says, What happened to us? She turns another page, and I wonder if crazy goes like this—back and forth, then and now, nothing absolutely sure about the stuff that happened.

There, she says, because she has found it at last—a photograph of a young man in a room of books and a single shining lamp. He is at work on a chipped library table, shirtsleeves rolled to the elbow. His hair is thick and soft as a squirrel's tail. His eyebrows are two boughs of a pine tree, crashing. The lamp is bright and some other dusty light comes in, and it's like someone has said his name and he has just then turned, and maybe it was Katherine behind the camera, maybe someone else.

Smartest one at Penn, Katherine says. Knew everything before the rest of us did. That was him. Your dad.

On the back of the picture she gives me to hold it says *Greg. 1965.* He was always on the hunt for beginnings, Katherine says.

The red quilt with the gold threads falls from my lap and capes Katherine's shoulders. A year goes by, and it is sophomore year at Penn, 1966, and it is November, and now every page is blank until Philadelphia is gone and Florence is next, my father's flooded city. There are cars crashed into cars in the streets. There are the broken parts of bridges floating by, pots and pans in window boxes, mattress springs on balconies, a dead horse in a garden. Katherine keeps turning the pages, and the photos rain out—the flood is here, in that store, and there, in that girl's skirt, and there in the pile of paintings on the back of a truck. There are people rafting down the center of streets on the faces of thin tabletops. Katherine stops, closes the book, sweeps the pictures from the floor.

You must be tired, she says.

39

When I wake, there's the smell of chocolate rising. Under the one lit lamp in the room, Katherine is working—knocking the end of the flour out of a sifter, sponging the sugar off the counter, stacking measuring cups.

I thought you might be hungry, she says. Two plates. Two forks.

Nearly nine o'clock, she says.

She sits on the striped chair. I huddle beneath the red-gold blanket. She says there are things my dad has said and things my mom has said, and would it be all right if we talked a little about some of what has happened. I turn my fork around the plate, a slow dial. I watch the slow bruising of the skies. I look back at the blur of her. Everything is leaking.

Katherine stands. Walks away and comes back with a box of tissues. She takes my hands in her hands. She holds them until we can talk again.

Your dad says that you're having some trouble remembering things. Street names. Time. Your phone. That sort of thing. Is he right about that? she asks.

I nod.

He says there are promises you don't keep, secrets you do. Places you go, things you won't tell him. Days when you get lost.

It's—hard

—to talk. So many words in my head, broken words on my tongue.

Yes, she says. Let's talk about how this began.

I take a deep breath. I say it: With a finch.

She leans back in her chair, lets my hands go, folds hers up beneath her chin. *What* would you say started with a finch?

Whatever—this is. Whatever I'm—

be—coming.

And what is that, honey? What would you say you are becoming?

Not me.

Tell me, she says, about the finch.

I tell her about nests. I show her, with my hands, how they are made. Purse nests and mud nests and throne nests and thorns. Looms and weaves and pockets. With the loosened threads of the quilt, I show her. With the spill of paper clips. With the blank pages of a journal book that is sitting on the table and the last of the tissues in the box and the glossy pages of magazines, their cover gloss. I tear them, weave them, round them, fold them; she watches, she lets me. Time passes and I don't know how much, I don't know why she doesn't stop me, how she can stand me, how I look to her—this girl who builds nests. She is sitting here, when I finish. She has not gone away. She takes the nest from my hands and places it in hers. She turns it around and upside down and then balances it on her two palms. The paper clips run in a circle around the edge. The bowl is paper, glossies, thread. No tassel. It is impossible. It's me.

It's beautiful, she says.

I can't stop them.

Them? Where are the nests, honey? What have you made them with? How many?

Beneath the bed, I try to say. With stolen things, I show her, somehow. With the boy's flowers. The boy. Benedetto. I say his name. It takes forever.

She writes everything down. She takes a long time writing. When she looks at me her eyes are full.

A boy named Benedetto? she says.

I nod.

A beautiful name, she says. It means "blessing."

Mine means—hope.

Yes, she says. Your father told me. He also said, Nadia, that no one but you has seen this boy. That perhaps he's just a dream you've had. Is that a possibility?

No, I say. Nodefinitelynot.

She leans forward. She leans back and she doesn't judge, she doesn't blame me. I rub the tears out of my eyes with my fist and when I see clearly again, I see that her room is shipwrecked—torn faces in magazines, a trail of clips, paper shreds, all those books in the landslide mountain fallen even harder.

What do you suppose they mean, these nests? she asks.

Something whole, I try to say. Something sure.

How do they make you feel?

Calm. Afraid.

Those are two very different things.

Calm when I make them. Afraid because—I have.

I write some of this. I try to say it.

This is your secret, then.

Part of it.

What is the other part?

I can't tell—

I'll wait.

The difference.

It's okay.

Between knowing and imagining.

40

She makes the room with the crinkle bed my room. She pushes the furniture around and trades the paper for sheets and finds another quilt, lavender and blue. She has an old nightgown for me to wear and a pillow in an embroidered case, and she asks if I want tea, and I say no, so she brings me water in a tall glass, four ice cubes.

Ten o'clock, she says.

I've called your dad, she says.

Sleep, she says.

I listen to the birds outside. To someone singing. I close my eyes and when I open them, I see the tree outside, the poppy tree—the sun trapped in the glitter of the buckets and the poppies wild and big and a thousand green woodpeckers yaffling and settling down among the poppies, two thousand wings, one thousand red heads. And there is Maggie—on the highest branch, with her

Okay, she says. It's okay. Sweetie, I'm here.

Someone's crying. I feel Katherine's arms around me.

You don't have to say anything else, she says.

I'm crazy, I say.

Aren't I?

bright hair, singing. There is Maggie, miracle Maggie, among the birds, among the flowers, buckets like nests.

Look, she is saying. *Your own beautiful thing.*

Look. I made it for you.

Watch out! I shout. *Something's coming.*

A fire on its way. A bright blaze coming from the end of the street and turning the corner and hurtling fast—a red streak toward the tree and the poppies and the wings and everything beautiful and strange, and I say, *Maggie, watch it. Maggie—that's him.*

Somebody is shouting.

41

Nadia.

Nadia.

I feel a hand on my shoulder. A hand on my cheek.

I'm right here. Wake up. Shhhh. Sweetie.

Just a dream, she says.

He's real, I say.

You're here, she says, with me.

42

We sit on the living room couch not talking. She turns the nest I made with her paper clips and papers in her hand and gets up and makes us tea, cuts us each a slice of cake, sets one down on my knee.

It's difficult, she says. I know.

There are mounds of books on the floor. Dog-eared magazines. Notes. Photographs of my father young. She is wearing the same thing she wore yesterday, and she doesn't ask me questions. She watches me. Tells me to drink. Tells me it's chamomile, which was her mother's favorite. My mother, she says, was so angry at me when I went away to Florence. So disappointed. You are ruining your life, she said. But I wasn't. I knew that. My life was just getting started.

I was young, she says, just a bit older than you.

I nod. I know. My father told me.

We have to be who we are, she says.

I don't—Don't want to be—This.

I know, she says.

Idon'twanttobecrazy.

Shhhh, she says.

I wait for her to tell me what's next, to give this a name, to tell me the truth, but she watches me, holds my hand, tells me to have some cake, it was just a dream, we'll get some answers.

I don't know anything for sure, she finally says. But I'd like you to continue to stay with me, so that we can talk some more. All right? I'd like us to work on this together, Nadia, and I'm asking the advice of some friends. Would you be all right with that? How does that sound?

I think of Mom and Dad and Jack at the Vitales'. I think of all the things that don't belong, and all the things I've taken. The museum of nests beneath the bed. The beautiful strange. The shipwreck in the Barbie sheets. The sad bald lonely bookbinder and the chain I stole from Perdita. The boy who is real. I have to see him.

I need to—go, I say.

Nadia, I can't let you do that.

I have to know—ifheisreal.

I'm not so sure, Katherine says. I'm not so sure that is a good idea.

She stands up, crosses the room. She stands there at the window, watching the world like my father watches the world, like all the answers we need are out there floating.

It's important, I say.

I promise tocomeback, I say. I won't leave again, justletmedothis.

She sits back down in her chair for a very long time. She studies me.

Can I trust you, Nadia, to return to me?

I nod.

Can I absolutely trust you? Tell me.

Yes.

I have two phones, she says. A house phone, and a cell phone. I'm giving you the cell phone, and if I need to call you, you will answer. If it starts getting late, I will find you, I will bring you back. You understand?

I nod.

Don't let me down, sweetie. I've been trusted with you.

I prom—ise.

This is the first and the last time, she says.

I nod.

She slips her hand into her pocket, finds her cell, cues up her house number, gives me a long hug.

I'll be right here waiting, she says.

I'mcomingback, I tell her.

43

A leather shop in the basement of the cathedral. That's what he said. Leather shop. Cathedral.

The hour is nine bells. I walk the plaza of Santa Croce. I find the dungeon doors. I hurry.

Past the well of light, down a few steps. Past a marble Christ wearing a crown of thorns. Now the hallway turns and becomes a long stone tunnel, green and gray, then red, until suddenly I am standing in an interior garden, and I think of Katherine at the top of the hill.

We're going to work on this.

Sun on my skin. The smell of olives. The sound of machines. The dull echo of a hammer, and now, at last I'm here: the garden of leather. I'm here. It's real. I'm not completely crazy.

The garden of leather is a two-story well built of scrubbed-yellow brick. There are potted trees on the thick stone paving and cut eyebrow arches along the low first windows, a fraction of sky, two cats. Beyond the windows in the rooms that run along the courtyard are long wood tables, sewing machines, needles, calf's hide, snakeskin, an old man, and, beside him, his head buried in his work, Benedetto.

I have found him.

There.

See?

Proof.

SCUOLA DEL CUOIO, a sign says. Private. Don't enter.

I hear a voice and turn. A woman with silk hair and eyes the size of cameos is coming close. She's talking.

She wants to know if I'm here for a tour. I tell her no. She wants to know if I'm here for the leather and I say no. She asks me my name. Nadia. She tells me hers. Laura. Says she is her father's daughter, and I don't know what she means or why she's said so, but I say, somehow, in words she understands, that I am my father's daughter too. What she really means, she says, is that her father was Marcello Gori, and this Scuola del Cuoio was his, and that for sixty-five years, in this Santa Croce annex, the Gori family has been teaching leather and selling what they make to the famous and to the locals and to the tourists.

That's Carlos, she says, pointing out the older man in the blue shirtsleeves. That's Carlos, but in the vaulted room, I see only Benedetto, working with his head tucked in close to a machine, his jacket slung across the back of his chair.

Turn, I think. But he doesn't see me.

In the courtyard the fattest cat rolls to its feet and waddles our way.

You're here on exchange? I hear Laura now.

No.

For pleasure?

My father— I say.

The flood, I say.

Of course, she says, like a fifty-year-old flood is the reason all Americans come to Florence, like this makes perfect sense, like I do. Such a terrible thing, she says. That flood.

The cat is close now, arching its back, then slinking in to rub its fur against my leg.

See that line? Laura says. She points to a thin trail of discoloration on the courtyard wall. The flood was there, she says. The water that high. The whole place like a big pool—but I'm not listening, because finally in the garden of leather, Benedetto has looked up, he has seen me. He stands, comes to the door, crosses the courtyard, through the sun, and the cat yawns, lazy.

You're here, he says.

You're here.

I think he's real.

44

The workshop is cool. Its floor is chunks of stone. The ceiling is a vault of brick. There are forms and tools and pelts, the glue and the nails, the soft, exposed bellies of half-made purses, the inside-outs of wallets, stitched leather. By the sewing machine where Benedetto was working is a long strip of chocolate-colored leather. Into it vertical pockets have been sewn, a double row of dark red stitching that separates one pocket from the next. The whole thing is too long and wide to be a belt, too short and stiff to be an apron, too strange for me to guess what it is. I imagine twenty-four tiny birds choosing these pockets as their nests, filling them with seed and twig. I imagine the songs of those birds. The breeze in their wings. How safe and tucked in close.

You've been crying, he says.

Can we—go somewhere?

He looks around at the shop, the machines, talks to Carlos. He fits his tools into a pouch and hangs the pouch on a hook and now he pulls his coat from his chair.

Vieni con me.

Through the tunnel of stone. Into the sun. Above the Vespa *vroom*. He slices the streets. I wrap my arms around his waist and rest my cheek against his jacket, against the duffel strap.

The streets are long, broken, straight. I close my eyes and find the dot-to-dots my father used to make to keep us quiet on Sunday mornings when it was Mom's turn to sleep in late. He drew them on the cardboard part of notepaper pads—big red dots and purple numbers that we'd connect with glitter pens, the lines tangling up like some cat's cradle.

It's not even a real shape, Jack and I would complain when we were done, and Dad would make a fake big deal about how badly our imaginations had failed us. *Look again,* he'd say, and we could see it then—the tangled lines like starbursts or stream ripples or the scrabbled marks that gray squirrels would leave on Locust Walk after a snow. The Santa Croce neighborhoods are like the dot-to-dots, and I hold on tight.

On the far end of a medieval street, at a place between the rammed-in houses, an alley cuts through. Benedetto brakes and slows the bike and walks me like I am a girl on a pony. Above my head, more washed clothes hang. From down the street three girls with linked arms come singing. When their song stops the only sound is the water plunking off the shirtsleeves high on the line, plonking and slapping, and the sound of Benedetto's boots on the stones.

Benedetto knows the guys at the next corner. He knows the couple pushing their wheeled basket of fruit and onions over the rough stones of the street. He knows the cats. He knows people, and they know him; he is real. One more snaking street and now Benedetto stops at a house like all the other houses, except the window trim is a cranberry color and the whole face of the thing is sky blue.

This, he says.

Here.

He helps me onto the street and through the door. It is the middle of the morning on a sunny day. It is dark in this house of Santa Croce. It is one window, one crack of light, pictures hung crooked on the wall and plates piled by the sink, and finally, finally, I breathe.

Tell me, he says, what it is, why you've come, and I have no right words with which to tell him. We have come all this way, and I can't.

He wipes his brow with the back of his sleeve. He steps toward the alcove kitchen, where the refrigerator is the color of old mustard and wears a calendar like a hat and opens with a hard tug. He pulls a copper pot of soup from the smoky chill and warms it on the stovetop—cabbage, chickpeas, salted pork. He finds half a loaf of bread and two shallow bowls, spoons with round faces and slender stems, and now he sits beside me, the bowls in our laps, and he asks me nothing. It's just him and me, sitting and not talking, until he stands again, crosses into the kitchen again, and cracks black pepper into the soup. He stirs and cuts the heat. He brings the pot to where I sit, ladles more soup into our bowls, returns the pot to the stove, and now he sits, and we watch the room with all its broken things like we are watching a show.

His boots on the floor. The triangle of his elbow here beside me. His hair like a lamp in the dark. The silence fading in and out, and Benedetto is talking, far away, telling a story. His story. Three years, Benedetto says. Juliette, he says. His mother. A gardener. The survivor. Lupus.

He talks and sometimes I hear. He talks and I see Maggie in the tree and the sun trapped in the buckets and the wild poppies and the two thousand wings, the wreck of things, Katherine waiting. I see this room lit up with growing things and a mother dying: lupus. Remembering and imagining. Knowing and imagining. Is there any difference? Was there? Ever?

He leans so close. He kisses me.

I'm not whoyouthink I am, I manage.

Who do I think you are?

Idon'tknow.

See? he says. No worries.

Bene—

Shhhhh, he says.

He touches the lids of my eyes with a finger. I see an angel dangling from strings. I hear the clacking of her wooden limbs, the running of her beeswaxed feet, her wings flapping, flapping in the breeze.

45

I wake in a dark room, and he's gone.

    The dream that I have had is gone.

    The angel is gone.

    The bowls of soup and the pot are gone.

    The floor above me creaks.

    Katherine's phone does not ring.

46

When he pulls the curtains apart there's sun. A room like an antique shop. A chest of drawers with a drawer missing, cracks in the planks of the floor, fray at the edges, big things and small things, things without names.

My mama, he says, has something to tell you.

Vieni con me.

He helps me up. Leads me through the squeeze of the stairs. At the top of the staircase the hallway bends like the dip in a bow tie and the light rains in from three naked ceiling bulbs and I stand for a long time until I am almost sure that it is not another dream. Painted stalks on the walls. Painted trees. A map of branches and the heads of flowers that aren't flowers but brushstrokes of copper and yellow and pink.

There are forests above us, pointy-nosed bees, birds with too many wings. The floorboards creak when we walk. At the end of the hall the duffel bag hangs from a doorknob. I trace one painted branch into the canopy of the ceiling. I trace another back down to the floor. I circle the flower petals with one finger. None of the birds fly, and the bee can't sting. It's a short, crooked hall. It's an untrue garden. It's a psychedelic sky.

When we reach the end of the hall he leans in to kiss me. His lips on my eyelids and then on my lips, and now I feel his fingers low on my neck searching for the skin beneath my collar. I reach for his hair with my hand, the dark chip in his ear, and I will have this moment for all of time, I will not forget this, will not forget you, Benedetto.

I whisper, but he doesn't hear. He kisses my ear, looks down at my hands, the map of my hands, and kisses me. Now he turns the knob and opens the door and it's a room big as a bed and a window and a chair, a thin quilt of a thousand colors.

From the dark ceiling flowers are hung—the dried husks of sunflowers, lilies, ferns, Miniato red, the fresh violet blues—all of the flowers upside down, and if you could see. If I could bring you here. If you could hold it safe, for me. This: On the heavy cross-beams are painted roots and sprouts, the cracked shells of seeds, the one small skull of a bird, a chain of big-eared orchids. On the bed are books and magazines, a bowl and a spoon, a green sweater, a long orange scarf, a woman, her face like Benedetto's.

Nadia, Benedetto says.

Julietta, she says. And her hair is just like his.

She has four pillows at her back—four old velvet squares. She has big eyes on high-up bones, a riverbed neck, long arms in a gauze shirt, the quilt drawn to her waist like an every-color skirt.

When the wind wanders through the room's one window, the dry bells of the flower heads rustle, soft little songs. The violet smells violet. The pages in the old books blow back and forth, like the order can't matter in her stories anymore. Here is the end. Here is the beginning. Here is the middle again.

Sit with me, she says, her English like Benedetto's English, round on the edges. She touches a place on the side of her bed where nothing else is.

I told her you were something, Benedetto tells me. She wants to see for herself how you are.

I feel my face go hot.

So you like my garden? Julietta says.

Pazzesco, I say softly. *Crazy.* Or someone who sounds like me says. Softly. *Bello.*

Esattemente. Julietta glances across the room toward her son.

And my city? she asks. Do you like my city?

Florence is . . . confused, I say. Confusing.

Esattemente, she says again. When she smiles I see that her teeth are like Benedetto's, too little and so white. I see how tired she is too, how much work it is to sit here against the velvet squares, her whole world this one room and the forest garden Benedetto has drawn for her on walls she cannot see. His mother, a survivor. Something to tell me.

What have you done? she says now, lifting my hand into her hands. The tips of my fingers are still scarred and rough, like I have dug, barehanded, into a bucket full of pins.

Pazzesco.

I want to tell her about the finch and the egret and the turtledoves, the green woodpeckers and the nests. I want to tell her about the angel on strings. I want to tell her how it feels to weave in and out, to build, to make, to want, to try so hard, so very hard, to keep everything safe and whole, sheltered from the storm. I want to tell her that I'm losing things, that I can't stay here, that I will vanish, that I have come to say goodbye, that I love her son, or would have loved her son, and what, I want to know, is a survivor? How do survivors survive?

Tired, I whisper.

Amore sempre.

Scared.

Anche io.

I lean in and kiss her on the cheek. I lean back, close my eyes and I don't know how much time goes by.

It's time to say goodbye. The real things, the good things, the strange things, the gardens, the song of the birds in their nests. Time to tell the truth. Benedetto is real, but I am disappearing.

Pleasedonotforgetme.

47

I find her at the top of the hill, in the back of the house, in the walled-in patio. The big pots on the stone ledges, the grill in a corner, the black apron hung from a hook, the stack of magazines. Katherine with the phone in her hand.

She stands. Her blankets slip to the ground. She takes me into her arms, hugs me hard, says, I was just about to call.

She wraps me in a blanket. We sit, east to west, each of us quilted into our own chairs.

There are bits of sun. Freckles of light on her face. She lifts the hat on her head and her hair falls to its hem. You're shivering, she says.

I pull the blanket to my chin and close my eyes. I draw the air into my lungs. I put everything I have into the question I will ask, this thing that suddenly I must know and Katherine can tell me.

Is it true, I find the words, finally, about the flood? Fourteen thousand works of art? Sixteen miles of records? Four million books? Eighteen million cubic feet of debris? Everything destroyed? Everything rescued?

Florence, November 4, 1966, Katherine says. The city survives.

I open my eyes, see the cloth clouds above scuttling in, see the thoughts moving behind Katherine's eyes, a breeze ruffling the pages of her magazines. She collects her hair into a knot and then it falls.

What are we going to—

Do? I ask.

Somewhere down there the city blinks on and off. Somewhere down there Benedetto is sitting with his mother, beneath all the flowers he has stolen for her, in the room he has made for her, in the hope of surviving. He is sitting there. Real. High on the hill, I am with the Mud Angel. The American who came to Florence and fell in love and stayed, who knows something about the business of rescue.

Has your father ever told you the story of Cimabue's Christ? I hear Katherine say.

I nod. My hands in my pockets, my blanket to my chin.

You've seen it? she asks. In the refectory of the Basilica of Santa Croce?

I nod. I've seen it. Cimabue's Christ is a work of art, fourteen whole feet tall. It is painted on two timbers planed from trees axed down in the Casentine Forests seven hundred years ago. I know this. I've seen it. I listened to that story.

The basilica took a lot of water, Katherine is saying, on the day of the flood. Eight feet. Nine. No one knows. Sheets of music were stuck to the ceilings. Bibles were crashed against the stones like bricks. Cimabue's Christ was so flooded out that the only way to reach it was by way of pontoons. The paint had burst from Cimabue's canvas—rained down like specks of fireworks. White lead. Cinnabar. Lapis. Gold.

Impossible to fix, I say.

Nothing's impossible.

This is. I am.

Some said the same thing about Cimabue's Christ, she says. Some people said to let it go, that the flood was too big, that it could not be fought. But the monks didn't listen; they had hope. They leaned over the edges of their little boats in the basement of the cathedral and scooped the flakes of Cimabue's face into tea strainers.

Cimabue had painted his Christ on a canvas, Katherine says. He'd hammered the canvas into the cross. He had used eight layers of gesso and the yolks of eggs and so much gold, and by the time the floodwaters receded the cross was three inches longer than it had been—the old wood saturated and swollen, splintering apart.

It took fifteen men to break the cross from its wall. It took fifteen to lay it facedown on the benches of the church, where it stayed until they carried the cross that had lost its Christ to a flatbed truck. It was driven over the river and to the top of the hill, to the Pizzi Palace. It was carried into Limonaia of the Boboli Gardens, where the Medicis had once grown their citrus trees.

It has grown cold up here on the hill. Katherine pulls the second blanket up to my chin and goes inside and finds a coat and comes back out with two glasses of tea.

Have some, she says.

Listen, she says. To the end of my story.

She says that word went out that Cimabue's Christ was gone. She says that after eighteen months they tied it to a flatbed truck and drove it to the old fort near the train station where, at last, the swollen timbers dried. They dressed the cross with Casentine timbers. They rearranged the canvas. They chose their paints. His face was in tea strainers. His limbs were swollen. And still, among some, there was hope. Women working in pearls. Men painting with squirrel-tail brushes. The work going on for years, one quarter inch at a time.

She says it took ten years, but Cimabue was saved. Nothing is impossible, Nadia. Nothing.

The day has turned to dusk. The pages of Katherine's abandoned magazines rustle like wings.

One thing at a time, she says.

One thing by one thing by one thing.

Trust yourself to trust me.

48

Into the bed, she says.
    Sleep, she says.
    Don't leave me.
    Don't forget me.
    A white room.
    A painted garden.
    Christ's face in a tea strainer.
    I'm not leaving, she says.
    Sleep.

49

This is the dream. The last thing I can tell you with the words that rush and break.

I have a key in my hand. A door clicks open. A hallway smells like motorbikes and boots. There is a woman standing by the mail slots. She is young. And pale.

She wears a dark wrap with three bright, round buttons. She puts a flame to a cigarette, pinches the lit match between blue nails. She nods but doesn't move. She exhales the first cloud of smoke, which hangs dense between her and me and the mail slots and the motorbikes and the heavy smell of gasoline in the entrance lobby.

Sleep, someone says.

Ciao.

Ciao.

Sleep. Only a dream. The woman with the blue nails, smoking.

Third floor, she says, tilting her chin up toward the rooms where she lives.

Second floor, I say. The Vitales'.

She knows. She pulls on her cigarette and releases its heat. She exhales and I see a tiny dog, white and fluffy, tucked into the crook of her arm. I see the tall shoes with the spiked heels in the shadows. I see the bookbinder's ribbons, like streamers, in her hair.

You're the one with the piano, I say.

Si.

I hear you, I say. In my sleep.

Si.

What is your name?

Agnese.

I didn't mean it, I say. I didn't mean to steal the pink. I didn't mean—

Tock.

—togocrazy. To leave everyone I love. To leave myself. I didn't mean for the nests not to save me.

Her eyes are olive-colored, and not serene. She rests her head against the wall and closes her lips in a silent hum. It's as if she has nowhere to go, as if she has been waiting for me.

Sleep, someone says.

She takes another drag of her cigarette. She exhales. The dog blinks beneath two furry eyebrows. They used to come and visit, she says. Those Vitale girls. They liked my songs.

She lifts the dog from its warm, tucked place and presses its nose to hers. It bleats and sticks its little pink tongue through its teeth. She says something and I see her lips move but my ears don't catch on the nouns. She takes another drag on her cigarette, tucks the dog back into its warm cove, gives me another long look. A column of ashes falls from her cigarette and she disappears, through the door, into the night of Florence, the lights of Florence, all the people gone, and I hear someone crying on the floor above, in the rooms that belong to the Vitales.

It's all right, someone says. I've brought another blanket. Here. Shhhhhh.

Someone is crying. Someone is hurt. I run through the lobby and up the stairs and the door to the Vitales' is open, a wind blowing through. The chairs and the couch and the table are gone, Jack and Dad and Mom are gone, the diary and the key are gone, and here, instead, is a forest of trees and leaves and ivy, tubs of ivy, curtains of ivy, buckets and buckets of poppies. There are nests built out of mattress springs and rubies, nests built out of hats and twigs, a nest built out of the hush and the mush of the moon, nests built out of flowers, feathers, ribbons, chains. *Tock.* There are two little girls, identical girls. There are two girls, and now, when they see me, they are running, they are leaving their whole lives behind.

Careful, I call. Careful! Watch out! Wait! But they run— through the trees, beneath the nests, toward the open window, they run, flapping and crying.

Shhhhhhhhhhhhhhhh.

Another blanket.

Here.

Four hundred billion birds in the world.

One finch.

Help me.

ANOTHER THING GAINED

It's always damp, or it will be soon. It grows dark, and the lights they string across the street tip in. People use their long umbrellas like walking sticks; everyone has three legs in Florence. The decorated tree beside the Duomo seems this side of squat when you're far away, and then you get up close, and it's like, wow, you can't even see to the top.

Once the snow made it all the way to the ground. I was in the piazza and looked up, and first I saw the snow sticking to my eyelashes and then I saw the people of Santa Croce jamming their windows up and ramming their sweater arms out and catching the flakes with their fists. It was truly YouTube-viral-worthy. A girl ran to kiss the shoes of Dante, left little swoosh tracks with her boots. The smaller kid who ran after her swished across the swoosh, like she was being pulled on a sled. That was a good splice out of time, a gleaming of hope.

In the wedding shop the dresses are vanilla frosting. In the jewelry shop all the velvet collars are red and the only necklaces on display are emerald-stoned. Every church has its own manger scene, leaving Jesus to get born every day. People sing here—spontaneous song. They drink prosecco like it's juice and there are long lines for hot chocolate at the Caffè Rivoire. This guy goes around with a saxophone, playing carols sweet.

But only once did it snow all the way to the ground.

I felt Ivy League–smart, bringing my tapestry coat—cornflower blue and rust, braided rope frogs instead of buttons, braided rope on its cuffs and double hems. I guess you could say that it's a little long and I should have tailored it, but the truth is when I walk up or down, and there's a lot of up or down in Florence, it gives me an excuse to go royal, to scrunch the fabric up with my hands, like a princess with a train, to teach these Florentines about Second Mile Style. Coat royale, I call it—way superior to anything they sell on Via Tornabuoni, despite the obvious factoid that Versace is cool, and so are Prada and Bulgari, and Ferragamo is so very prime that it has its own museum in the Palazzo Spini Feroni. But wherever I go, whenever it is, I wear my coat royale.

It's wetter than cold; it's always wet. There are all these old bones planted in the earth—monk bones, nun bones, priest bones, genius bones, even the bones of Dante's first crush. You feel their souls wafting up, getting stuck on your boots, your tights, your socks, on the hem of your coat. I asked Perdita how she stands it, and first she smiled, and then she looked at Jack, and then he translated, and she stopped smiling. You are born for it, Jack said, she said. Born for the weather, I think she meant, but that's not what I was asking. My question was: How do you stand all the bones of the dead, everywhere you go, beneath your feet?

They do a very fine roasting of chestnuts here—*bruciate*. I stand by the fire, the smoky waft. I try to remember all the words on my burgeoned vocab list: excitatory, inhibitory, medulla oblongata, dorsolateral, orbito, ventromedial prefrontal. Katherine says I should make it easy on myself. Start with the four lobes of the cerebral cortex: occipital, temporal, parietal, frontal. Start with the neuron: cell body, axon, dendrites. Start with recognizing just how difficult this all will be to grasp: 100 billion nerve cells in a three-pound brain. The mind folded in on itself.

Anything could happen.

Florence goes up. Florence goes down. Like the steam above the pots and pans that Jack and Perdita command. They can't help themselves. Those two.

We go to Nadia in the early afternoon—one-thirty, two o'clock.
We walk side by side, our hands in our pockets, my iPad in my
wicker purse, and mostly we don't talk, except for when one of
those at-risks comes up. I'll be eating my chestnuts and she'll be
talking, and it's like the at-risks are Mrs. C.'s parables, her object
lessons. They're her proof.

The runaway comes home.

The dyslexic wins the scholarship.

The cutter stops stealing her father's razor blades and finally
stops cutting herself.

The OCD germaphobe takes the subway every afternoon to a
part-time job in the station mall on Market.

And always last, in the stories, she tells, some guy named Amir
sees it through.

"Amir," she says. Cracking a borrowed chestnut.

There's a girl who waits for us every day—five or six years
old, always the same red sweater on. Sophia Loren lips. A pair of

beat-up cowboy boots. She lives in a house on the hill across from Belvedere. She must sit in the window waiting for us, because as soon as we're close, she's there. Pops out of the front door with a gappy smile on her face. Our own welcoming committee, and good Lord, given the way things are, we can use a welcome in triplicate.

"*Buongiorno*," she says.

"*Buongiorno*."

Popping back out of sight and closing the door like some Ambassador of the Hills. I crack a chestnut.

We get three hours in most days. Intensives, we call them. We do the life work, the focus work, until the third hour winds down, or until doing more will hurt more than stopping where we are. Almost every day we do it—leave the apartment, cross the river, make the climb to Katherine's house, settle in for the intensives with Nadia. Two weeks ago, two days in a row, there was too much storm and we couldn't go, and those two days were the saddest days of all, holed up in the apartment on Verrazzano, listening to the piano playing upstairs like a dirge. Nothing we could do. No hills. No intensives. No nouns. No Nadia. My best friend in the world. My community garden assist.

We had ourselves a plan.

At night I keep up. I've switched over to the MOOCs for now. Massive Open Online Courses—a bunch of videos and message boards and crowdsourced e-buddies; ask a good-enough question and it climbs the board and the prof slaps you back with an answer—live. I'm not saying that this beats shoulder-to-shoulder in the classroom, but it's where I'm at right now, how I remain "academically greedy" (my parents' favorite term). I stayed local with my MOOCs—signed up for the Penn-proffed, Quaker love and whatnot:

1. Design: Creation of Artifacts in Society
   (Professor Karl Ulrich)
2. Pay Attention!! ADHD Through the Lifespan
   (Professor Anthony Rostain)
3. Modern and Contemporary American Poetry
   (Professor Al Filreis)
4. Basic Behavioral Neurology
   (Professor Roy Hamilton)

I'm greediest of all for number 4.

Jack, when he's not cooking, not reporting back on his spices, keeps up his work on the opus magnum: *Brunelleschi Rising*. Almost Independent Study 201. Studying the old books, Binging the net, going out and asking questions of old-timers in Italian, then coming back to the flat and plumping the room with his repertoire of new-to-his-own-self facts. "Did you know," he will say, about the Santa Maria del Fiore and its famous biggest-in-the-world arched cap, "that no one thought it'd be possible to build a Duomo like that?"

"Knew it, Jack."

"That years and years and years went by before anybody tried?"

"I read the *Lonely Planet*."

"Did you know that there are seventy million pounds of marble, brick, and stone up there, all of it supporting itself?"

"Now I do."

"They built it on air."

"You mean on top of the air."

"Called it a nest of delights. Called Brunelleschi crazy until they called him a genius instead."

"Way of the world, I guess."

"Had it bad until he had it good. It happens. Right? It happens. Anything can."

"Happens."

Brunelleschi Rising. Jack's thesis in a nutshell. His new proof of hope.

We sit when Jack goes on. It takes a moment before the dirge dies down. The bells in the bell towers chime. The ivy leaves chase each other's tails, run through the silver stop signs of the Vitale thumbtacks. And then it will be dinnertime, and we'll sit there close, at the Vitales' table, and spew signifying metaphors.

(A phrase I picked up in the Poetry MOOC.)

Little-known fact (courtesy of Jack): There's a subterranean river running through the soils of Florence, deep beneath the Duomo. A whole river down there that nobody sees, running on and on, and every day, tourists climb the tourist steps and think they are safe, high above.

(Nobody's safe.)

Little-known fact (courtesy of the prof): After the floodwaters of 1966 were gone, there were half a million tons of mud in the streets of Florence, and guess how many citizens? Precisely. Easy math. One ton of mud to every person in Florence. And the mud got good and gone.

(Hope can be found.)

Little-known fact (courtesy of at-risks): In some cities in the United States as many as 60 percent of high school students ultimately drop out. If you start looking for the signs when the students are sixth-grade-young you can help them beat the rap. Early intervention. That's the key.

(It's right there, end of story: Early intervention is the key.)

Little-known fact (courtesy of Perdita—Perdita with the cable-knit tights and the green feather earrings and the spice tricks, the spice facts, the jars of this and that): The history of spice is the history of the world, and where there is history, there is future.

(We believe.)

Little-known fact (courtesy of me): The hundred billion nerve cells in the three pounds of folded brain are not fixed. They are plastic; they remap. *Voilà*. Dr. Roy Hamilton, MOOC Number 4, calls the brain a masterpiece. He says, looking straight and directly at me through the screen, that the brain—my brain, yours, anybody's—harbors "a near-infinite capacity for connectivity." He says "beautiful" and "complicated," and in terms of the future for people in some kind of brain trouble, we're only staring at the tip of the berg.

(Nothing is fixed, and nothing is certain.)

Dinner at the Vitales' is metaphors time. It's when we hope out loud.

Dr. Katherine Goldrath is a Dr. Roy Hamilton fan. Sometimes, at her house on the hill, she watches the MOOC videos on my iPad, and sometimes she talks back, disagrees, reaffirms, proposes, *what if?*, until I say, "Not like he can hear you, Katherine." She'll flip her long white hair to the opposite shoulder, press her fingers to the skin beneath her eyes, get up, cross the room, power up her own computer, and tap out an e-mail directly to Dr. Roy because she's in the brain business and can. "Professional discourse," she'll say, about their relationship. Leaves it at that.

She offers lemon squeezed into seltzer water. She offers cookies from a red tin, ginger tea. She keeps a window open, even with the rain, and when the intensives are done and all the cards put away and it's quiet in the front room across from Belvedere, she leans back and tells us about the news inside her magazines, or stories from before, when she was still a practicing head doctor. The paralyzed man learning to walk. The lady born with half a brain in full alert and thriving. The congresswoman shot close-range in the head by a demented man who talked and walked again.

Also: Barbara Arrowsmith-Young, who, young, couldn't tell time, couldn't compute relationships, couldn't get the irony knack, couldn't even figure out, when she touched a stove with her left hand, where the pain was coming from. Barbara Arrowsmith-Young had so many problems that her own mother said she'd be dead real soon.

Almost, but not. Even when she tried to take her own life, she failed at that, too, until at last she found a way to change herself. To teach her brain to overcome its broken parts. She taught her brain clocks. She taught her brain maps. She taught her brain irony and style. She taught her brain philosophy. She forced her brain to do new things until it reshaped itself—built itself new neuronal networks to bypass the ones that didn't work.

I picture train tracks. I picture tree roots. I picture tree branches tangling in the sky. I picture Barbara Arrowsmith-Young and her brain-training, an Olympian of the mind. I hear Katherine finishing her news in the house on the hill: Knowledge, she's saying. Optimism. Parallels and metaphors. We fight our war like that.

I look past her, past the kitchen, through the open door toward the white, white room with the glass shelves. I look past her and see Nadia's hair tumbling off the bed, falling away from itself.

It hardly ever snows in Florence, but man, does it rain. We walk away from Belvedere when it's already dark—me and Mrs. C. The little girl in the red sweater and cowboy boots watches us through the front-room window of her brown-yellow house.

She cheers us on.

I could have been her. Once. I wish I could show her the angel that Nadia found in the shop called Curiosities. How it dangles from strings. How it dances in the breeze. How it says *hello, hello*. How it has wings.

I sleep in the top bunk, in the Barbie pinks. The piano songs fall. Paganini, Caprice No. 24, sometimes. Sometimes Christmas carols and sometimes old rock and roll, give us a little Carly Simon. Please. There's dog yip up there and some mean stiletto heels. When I take a deep, long breath, I do an intake of sticky glue. When I dream, I hear the chip-chip sound of scissors.

From the very start, in the morning hours, I've returned the things Nadia stole. It's like detective work, archaeological, its own kind of intensive—matching the things laid across the floor to the places they might have come from. One of those kaleidoscopes that splits the color world to fractions. A couple of satin pillows with tasseled ends. A dozen scarves. Rosaries and garlic chains, felted buttons, leather twists. One rubber glove the color of a baby's duckie. A box made out of leather, pretty papers, stamps. And glitter. And ropey chains. And a piece of broken glass.

Faded flowers.

Nadia could have owned her own shop, the way she was going, and I don't always win the match-to-match. But if I were taking a class called the Shops of Florence, I'd be so ace they'd have to give out a triple-A-plus. Taddei made the leather box in his shop across from what they claim is Dante's house. Alice on Via Faenza had the bright pots of glitter. All the books Nadia stole from Paperback Exchange, the best little bookshop in Florence. The best scarf of the lot was lifted from L'Elefante Verde, and on the day I went in bearing my she-didn't-mean-to-steal-it gift, Loriana Bergantini, the owner of the shop, did a little courtesy bow and called me honorable.

Nadia's honorable too, I wanted to say. Nadia's just not Nadia. Right now. Nadia, mostly, is fighting.

In Le Telerie Toscane, they were grateful. In the shop along the Ponte Vecchio, they called me the dubious American. In Del Moro they took me on a tour of all the hats—the merino wool, the straw, the leather—and showed me where the chartreuse silk had been stolen from. *Keep it,* they said. *Keep it. We understand.* That was the hardest return of all, and for that return, I took Jack's friend Perdita, whose style is totally rad.

I have my system worked out—easier to harder. I am up to the fourth tier, the match-to-matches I hadn't scored on yet. Scarves that could have been sold by any one of the ten dozen street vendors. Flowers sucked dry of their colors. Lily souvenirs that might have been snatched out of any unsuspecting tourist's purse. An old-style Timex, ticking like a bomb, that I hadn't hooked up with one of the two million antique shops or (perhaps) a grandfather's pocket. A gold chain, screwdriver-thick, practically padlocked together at its ends, its pendant broken. I found the chain one day when Perdita was near. She saw it in my hands. She gasped.

"My chain," she said. "My chain. It's here." And then she looked for Jack.

I've arranged Nadia's nests on the twins' bottom bunk like a private museum. Nadia's nests, her beautiful, bold nests—her *Goodnight Moon*, her sunflower soufflé, her tornado weaves and her potholder looms, her stolen jewels, the perfect mattress spring, the dried husks of flowers that are so dried now I don't even know what they were. It's as if the birds themselves had taught Nadia their secrets—the hoisting and weaving, the cementing and sculpting, the majesty magic of mud and spider silk, the pillowing down. I would have gone blind making those nests—even just one. I would have lost my fingers inside the tangles and silks, given up, gotten out, but not Nadia. Nadia persisted. She persevered. She *compulsed*. That's one of the words Dr. Hamilton uses when he talks about cases like hers, and one of the words that I hold in my head when I stand at the window of this borrowed room and look out. The waiters, the girls, the faded stucco, that glass room where a man works behind a taped-up window. Sometimes he looks up and I wave, but he never waves back. He turns out the light. He checks the seams on the tape in his window.

There are four dozen MoMA-worthy nests in the bottom bunk in the twins' room in the Vitale flat. There are four dozen nests, and they are gorgeous, each one, and maybe that's what hurts most of all, in all this.

Nadia. Our artiste. But the art is a disease. Nadia's mind is a fog.

She thinks in full sentences, Katherine explained, when I asked her, when I said I could not understand. But she cannot find the words on her tongue. A catastrophe in expressive language. Complicated by obsessions, memory lapses, delusions.

What kinds of delusions?

She can't tell us. Right now.

The prof blames himself. Says he should have seen it, should have known, should not have brought his family here. What is an obsession? he asks. What is a disease? What is a choice, and what is an affliction? He has a *PhD*. He's a *historian*. He is an *Ivy League* man. All this time in Florence, searching for the place where chaos began—the flood. All this time, and it was right there, climbing the steep hills beside him.

Mrs. C. says, "Shhhh, let's be strong." Mrs. C. says, "One day at a time. The science is progressing. Look at how well she is doing. Look at all we can do for her now. Listen to Katherine."

"She's in the best hands."

"She is young."

Mrs. C. is there every day, in the house where Katherine lives and Nadia has been staying since the middle part of October, when she could no longer return to the nests she loves and the nests that torment her. Obsessive thoughts. Disinhibited behaviors. Delusions. Loss of expressive talk. I keep trying to get the words right. To see past the labels. To understand the stories they tell me, to understand this man—Dr. Bruce Miller at the University of California, San Francisco, whom Katherine says is the best they have. A neuroscientist-philosopher with answers. A doctor who listened when Katherine called.

"Bring her here," Dr. Miller said.

Over and over, in our walks up the hill, Mrs. C. tells me what Dr. Miller said. During the quiet hours in the apartment. During the mornings when we stop at a church and sit in the quiet together. During the evenings when Jack cooks, when Perdita helps him, Mrs. C. talks. She tells the story of Dr. Miller and the diagnosis.

In San Francisco, they tunneled Nadia into the MRI. They asked her to wear the EEG hat. They named fifteen things—milk, paper clips, cell phone—and wrote down which Nadia remembered and how long her remembering took. They showed her pictures of animals and asked what they were. They gave her denotation tests, connotation tests, quizlets on pejoratives, sarcasm, satire, parody, irony. They asked her to draw a clock, draw a flower, copy a picture built out of lines and spokes.

Then they asked her to reproduce her own nests, to explain what she could about the birds. *Why the birds, Nadia? What about the finch?*

They did all these things, according to Mrs. C., and then they told a story about a man named Maurice Ravel—French, an impressionist, a hooligan, a small man in meticulous clothes, a composer. Most people know Ravel for his composition called *Boléro*—two melodies arranged on top of a repeating snare drum rhythm. Two melodies only, repeated again and again, played first by flute, then by clarinet, then by bassoon, until finally every instrument in the entire orchestra is in on the game—the same two melodies, the same on-and-on drums. Perseverative. Systematic. Rigid. *Compulsed.*

"Why are you telling me this?" Mrs. C. said. "Why all this talk about a composer?"

"Because Nadia may be like him in some ways," Dr. Miller said. "She may have the condition Ravel may have had."

"Which is?"

"Frontotemporal dementia, primary progressive aphasia."

"But Nadia's young."

"Yes."

"You said *dementia.*"

"I did."

"Dementia is Alzheimer's. It's old people."

"Not always, Mrs. Cara. Not in some very rare cases, it isn't."

Dr. Miller had a model of the human brain on his desk—a plastic version of mental cauliflower. He showed Mrs. C. the front left, the language center. He showed her the right, a node in the back, the visual and spatial processing department. "The scans," he said, "are suggesting that, in Nadia's brain, the language center is shrinking. They're suggesting, too, that the part of the brain that generates art is growing, gaining weight, thriving. One thing lost and another thing gained. A brain rearranging itself.

"The plastic brain," he said.

"Art as the mind's great disinhibition," he said.

"The erupted artiste," Mrs. C. said. The erupted artiste. Our Nadia.

There are others out there, with what Nadia might have—that's what the doctor said. A couple hundred sudden painters, sudden landscape designers, sudden musicians—these ordinary people who, little by little, become less of themselves and more of something lovely-strange, their words and inhibitions going away as their artwork flowers. There are experiments being done with some kind of machine that changes the magnetic field inside the brain and temporarily creates brain states just like Nadia's. The volunteer subjects become insta-artists for an hour. Their one thing lost, their other thing gained.

But for them, the lucky ones, it's temporary.

The Caras spent a week in San Francisco. They spent a week, and then they returned. To Katherine, on the hill. To the Mud Angel and the blessed.

I want to go
home,

Nadia said.

And every time they asked Nadia what home was, she said, or tried to say, Vit—. Vita—. Santa—. She said, or tried to say, something else, too.

Nobody understood the second something. Everybody understood Florence.

I'm here because Nadia asked, because one day after all those days my phone finally buzzed and it was her. All those weeks gone by, all my e-mails and no answers, texts and no answers, days I was sure she'd forgotten.

"Too good for me now, Nads?" I'd started to say, to the quiet zone of my phone. "Too big for her own Italian britches," I kept saying, to my mom, who told me to leave it alone, to think bigger than mad, to remember that people can struggle. I made a new friend at Penn, a guy named Denny. I went out photo hunting with him and I stole into the med school pond with him and I took him Clark Park shopping and I gave him some peas from my garden and I let him kiss me and I didn't bother texting the news because he wasn't that great anyway and two weeks later he wasn't my friend. I didn't tell Nadia any of that. She was too far away. She was gone.

Then, early November, that text came in, five words: I *need* yu plese com. No yellow smileys and no bouquet of red hearts and more spelling mistakes than my Ivy-League-at-fourteen best friend had ever made in her responsible life.

About an hour after that, Mrs. C. called. About an hour after that, I was on a Skype call with Nadia's new friend. Meet Katherine, Mrs. C. said. And there was Katherine—one of those women with very white hair whose face is so young you're sure she's white-bleached her glorifying tresses. About an hour later and my mother and father were on the phone too, and it was settled and the tickets came, courtesy of the Caras.

I had three days. Packed myself. Tarped up my garden. Got on the plane in Philly, watched the seagulls in the sky, took off, didn't sleep, flew into Rome, trained into Florence. Met the prof and Jack on the Florentine track. Hustle and bustle, like a Hollywood film.

"You must be tired," the prof said.

"I want to see her," I said.

The prof ran his hand through his wild hair and pressed on his eyebrows and decided.

"Jack," he said, "take Maggie's suitcase to the flat."

"Now?"

"Yes."

"But I . . ."

"Now, Jack."

Jack fit his hand into the suitcase handle, scowled but didn't look back, and Second Mile Style rolled east, through the painted city toward the lantern of the Duomo, which I'd already read about in *Lonely Planet* on my plane ride here.

The prof and I took a circular south. Past the first church near the train station, past its piazza. Past the Grand Hotel Minerva, down the Via del Fossi. To the Lungarno Corsini and over the Ponte Vecchio and up the Costa dei Magnoli to the Via di Belvedere. I'm big on names. It was about eleven in the morning Florence time. I was blister-toed and disoriented, despite my pre-studying all the maps.

They call Philadelphia and Florence sister cities, but there is nothing in their DNA that comes close to even a species match. Philadelphia is squares and grids, predictable angles, flat. Florence is Spirograph swirls and little-kid squiggles, roads that change names just like that, a sturdy set of climbs. I was glad every time the prof had to stop. I'd turn, try to get a view, suck in some breath.

"We're grateful to you for coming," the prof said.

"She's my best friend," I said.

"She's my primo."

Both of us standing there catching our breath.

It was misting in Florence. I could feel my blisters split and peel inside my patent-leather boots—with buckles, seventies style. I could feel my thumbs and pinching fingers cramp in the folds of my coat. That Belvedere wall is one hell of a wall—worse than the henchman Jaws in *The Spy Who Loved Me*, another seventies giant. We approached it from the west. We stair-climbed and angle-stalked. And then we got to Katherine's. Just as pretty as she was on Skype. And just as super kind.

Nadia's thinner. Nadia's dark hair is so long and her skin's white as photographic paper before it takes its bath and her eyes are blacker than ever. It was cold and her thin feet were bare, but she was there at the door when I arrived. She'd heard me calling for her, because I'd started calling to her, because the prof had said that we were close—just a bend in the fortress wall from her now.

Katherine's house is square and sweet, short as a stunted tooth. There are candles in the window, a bunch of plaster *Davids*, two potted evergreens by the front door, the two pots bowed up in gold. In the door, in the mist, between the candles, between the gold, Nadia stood like that angel on strings. She wore an old sweater, a pair of turquoise jeans.

"Don't—leave—me," she said, wrapping her arms around me, tight.

"Look at me," I said, pulling back, finding her eyes—dark but also burning with light. "I am Maggie Ercolani. I am right friggin' here. I am your best friend. Always."

That first day in the house on the Belvedere hill, we didn't let a crack of sad break through us. I knew what I had to do, what they were counting on me to do—me bringing Nadia stories, whole. "Narrative continuity," Katherine had said, in the pre-trip Skypes, when she was preparing me for now. "Your together stories." As if Nadia's remembering were a dot-to-dot, and my remembering were a pencil.

"Let your remembering be a pencil."

Katherine, who is so very modern, so still American, so kind to the old prof, said any story I had that could help keep Nadia framed and contexted was as good as medicine. She said to have them on the ready, not to be afraid just to talk. Nadia understands everything we're saying, Katherine said. The words go in fine. It's the words coming out that are harder. Receptive language. Expressive language. They're two different parts of the brain.

We sat in the sitting-room part of the house on the hill—Katherine and the prof in chairs and Nadia beside me on the couch, a little satin pillow in her lap, like a cat. I told Manakeesh stories—*labneh*, shawarma, *kafta*, *tawook*, lamb *lahm b'ajeen*. I told about the painted squirrels along Locust Walk, and the broken button ahead of old Van Pelt, and the Ethiopian restaurant with the blues on top.

"Nadia, remember that?"

I told about the sled in the snow and the poppies in the trees and the corn-husk maze, the river in the winter and the river in the summer, more bluegrass specials.

"Nadia, remember?"

I told about the big storm and the finch nest and the night we went sledding, and Nadia said, clear as day, even if the words were a little smashed: "World's greatest miracle." All the words all together, the little kitten of a pillow on her lap, and we laughed, and it felt so good that we laughed again, and out of nowhere and nothing I'd said, Nadia started to sing, waving her arm like a flag at the *Hurrah* like all true Quakers do.

Come all ye loyal classmen now
In hall and campus through,
Lift up your hearts and voices
For the Royal Red and Blue

Fair Harvard has her crimson
Old Yale her colors too,
But for dear Pennsylvania
We wear the Red and Blue.

"She's singing 'The Red and Blue,'" I said, and Katherine nodded, her eyes full as two cups of tea. "Yes," she said, "I know." Because (I know this now, thanks to MOOC Number 4) singing comes from another part of the brain than talking, and the singing wasn't gone for Nadia, and neither were the Quakers gone for Katherine, who left the campus fifty years ago.

We'd gone from laughing to crying, all for various causes, but we had not cracked to actual sad, and I was holding Nadia's hand, the scars on her hand, her scabbed skin flesh like the ridge on a crab. I was holding her hand, then running a stream of braids down her long, long hair, skinniest braids you've ever seen; I'm good at this. She kissed my cheek with the strength she had, and I started another braid near the top of her head, and Katherine's house smelled like warm cinnamon and raisins, and there were stacks of magazines, like Grecian columns all around.

And then Nadia was tired, and I was, too, and it was enough for one day. It was a lot. It was the prof standing, and then I stood, and fit my coat royale back on my bones.

"I'm coming back," I said.

"Don't—leave—"

"Look at me. Look at me hard. I'm coming back. I promise."

I left Nadia, on that first day in Florence, with six perfect braids zippering up and down her head. I left her there—the prof's primo student, Katherine's patient, my best friend. The prof and I went down the hill, east. We turned and went north. We crossed over the river Arno. The mist had turned to rain by the time we reached the Piazza Santa Croce.

"You're so good for her," he said.

Mrs. C. was the one who had picked the lock to the twins' room and opened the door and found Nadia's world the way Nadia had left it, while Nadia made her new home with Katherine. Everything blown to bits and upside down, bashed and collided, except for the nests, in the dark beneath the bed, taking shelter.

"It's like you see on TV after a storm blows through," Mrs. C. told me, after the prof and I had made our way to the Vitales', that first wet afternoon. "All the smash and unbelonging, the pieces that don't fit, and then suddenly the camera cuts to a rosebush with unbroken buds or a stack of plates without a chip or a photograph that got tucked inside a child's coloring book, not a tear or a ruffle. You don't know, when you see the footage after the storms, which is more impossible—the smash or the save. You don't know if order is more natural, or disorder. You don't know," Mrs. C. kept saying. "You can't imagine how it was."

Then she asked me to kneel before the bed, and I did, and she kneeled, too. She showed me the genius apparent in Nadia's museum of nests, the handwork and ingenuity, the craft of Nadia's miniatures, the intricacies, symmetries, deliberate deviations. There was the magnificent and there was the strange, zirconium-winking, little *ta-das*, like a Betsey Johnson necklace.

"Can you imagine?" Mrs. C. said, and I felt myself cracking with sad, but also wonder, and also eternal gratitude that they left the nests just as they were, thieving be damned.

There were fresh sheets in the top bunk of the twins' room. There were the accessories to the crime in the corner—all the unused paraphernalia that I'd soon start tiering out, returning to their owners. There was the cell phone, dead to the world. A pileup of texts inside, I'm sure.

"Thank you," Mrs. C. said. "For everything you're doing."

"Of course."

"For coming."

"She's my best friend."

"She has a chance."

"More than a chance."

"You'll help her. We know this. We're grateful."

I left the nests just as they were. I gave the Caras the comatose phone. I peeled the boots off my feet. I climbed up to the second bunk and lay there with my coat still on, buttoned to my chin like a tattered blanket, the mist still in its hem. I closed my eyes, and it was fall and winter, spring, and we were high in the eye of Franklin Field, for this was another Nadia plan. We'd stomped up the stadium stairs to the highest hot bench, and we were lying there, end of May, head to head, and Nadia said that she had something to say.

"Something bad?" I said.

"Something different," she said.

And I sat up and she lay there, saying nothing.

"What?" I asked.

"Things are changing," she said.

The sky was gallons and gallons of blue and a few clouds that she called hippo clouds and the scissor slice of a wing. Some runners were circling on the track below, some coach was blowing a whistle, and Nadia sat up and I started plaiting her hair, quick and even, starting at the top, by her skull.

"End of everything, will I always have you?" she said.

"What are you talking about?" I said.

"It's my dad," she said. "It's a grant. It's Florence."

And there was a hawk. And there was a crack above our heads.

And there were six braids like six zippers on her head.

These things I know, these things I had been told, these things MOOC Number 4 remind me daily, thank you, Dr. Roy Hamilton, thank you, Internet.

The brain is small, and it is capacious.

A stimulated brain is a yearning brain is a learning brain—more neurons, axons, dendrites, not to mention: a warmer bath of blood.

The imagination is strong enough to rearrange the anatomy of the brain itself—the stuff that happens within the cauliflower folds, the connections between neurons. Pay attention, beat it back, want something, insist, practice a new skill, and you forge a new thinking path. Ask a stroke victim, an OCDer, a diagnosed panic attacker, Barbara Arrowsmith-Young, the half-brain lady. You can think some brains toward whole. You can imagine past yourself. You can put a patch on your good eye to make your bad eye work. You can use your left hand to trace the lilt of Persian letters if your right brain is tricking you out. You can memorize long poems in a foreign language if you've stopped hearing as well as you should. If you slow down when you're writing with a pen, you'll elevate yourself into being a much more fluent reader.

I am not speaking, by the way, of fake science, or goo-goo myth. I am referring here to the proven stuff, the kind they prove with machines.

Until Dr. Bruce Miller can open his clinical trials for a pharma intervention for people who have what my best friend has, hauling Nadia's brain off to the brain-exercise gym is all that we actually have. The stories we return to. The games we play. The afternoon intensives. Nadia had come to Katherine and broken down. She'd had a nightmare about birds, she had confessed to everything, she had said that she could not go back to the nests she loved, that words were like dropped crumbs in the forest.

These things I know.

I also know this:

In the top drawer of the twins' desk there is a little-girl diary, its lock broken open. In the first pages, in thick gel ink, there is little-girl handwriting, in Italian. Sometimes the writing in pink and sometimes the writing in green, like the twins are one single person with one single secret stream, done up in two colors. All of a sudden, thirty pages in, the little-girl writing stops. The pages are blank, blank, blank, blank, and then there is writing again, one solo letter on every page, in scratchy, sticky ink:

B
E
N
E
D
E
T
T
O

Benedetto, Nadia's letters say. But no one I know has ever seen him.

In the afternoons the intensives. In the early evenings the MOOCs. In the mornings I try to figure out who Benedetto is.

This is part of what I'm here to do. This is what Nadia needs. She just hasn't had the words to tell me.

Maggie Ercolani. On a mission.

The clues as I have them, as I have dug them out or provoked them, planted them into the back blank pages of the diary with the busted lock and the gel-pen Italian and the word that ends in the circle of a nest:

There was a boy, maybe there was a boy, Nadia said there was a boy; no one has seen him. His name, if he exists, is Benedetto. His hair, if this is true, is bright as light.

(Courtesy of Katherine, who has begun to sleep on her sitting-room couch, which puts her closer, she says, to Nadia in the night. Closer in case Nadia dreams harder and needs her worse, in case she reveals more in her sleep, which is when she talks the most, when her language comes back to her, sometimes.)

Mrs. C. says she knows nothing about a boy. Prof says Nadia had secrets. *Someone was running.* Jack says there were plenty of times when Nadia went missing and the millions of things she never explained and the him she kept insisting on, so probably there's a boy, but Jack has never seen the boy. Perdita has said, her hair in different stripes each time she's said it, "This is Italy, where the love always lives."

"But have you seen the boy, Perdita?"

"No."

"Do you know a Benedetto?"

She shakes her head. There are a thousand Benedettos.

"Is there a boy, Nadia? A real boy?" I've asked my best friend ever, the plan-ness, and she has nodded, and she has said "steam" and "leather" and "flowers" and frankly, her clues don't help me much. I have said "Benedetto" and she has started to cry cry cry.

In the mornings, I'm on the prowl, keeping my eyes peeled. In the evenings, too, I spy. Walk down the streets and through the markets looking for an illuminated boy. They've brought the Weihnauchtsmarkt to the Piazza Santa Croce—hauled Christmas in from Heidelburg to sell German Santas and German crèche scenes, glühwein and wurst, stollen cake with thick white icing, poinsetta wreathes, Austrian strudel, dog bowls, candy in containers that look like Jetson-style hair dryers, embroidered tablecloths, pine-needle owls, wicker baby carriages. Germany in Italy for Christmas. This is the way of the world.

The pretzels hang from wooden clothes trees and the pom-pom hats are pinned upside down and the spices are sold out of burlap bags. Every awning is red-and-white striped, and every booth is lit, sometimes by candlelight, sometimes by Chinese lanterns shaped into stars. There's a pig on a spit and a live fire, a German band, metal chairs that are always wet, like the stones are always wet, like everything in Florence is drowning, memories of the flood, the prof says.

In the winter, in Florence, at night, it's all shadows. In the undersides of bridges. In the porticos of buildings. In the awnings and the domes and the rooftops. They string the holiday lights across the alleys—side to side, in a crisscross. They cable over like axons, tangle like dendrites. I keep wanting to forum this up in my MOOC—the representation of brain circuitry in the lights of Florence—but my comment is not getting crowdsourced. For now, then, I will simply share this with you:

The brain is inside the head, but the brain is outside, too. Every single place you look there's evidence of neurons.

"You go on ahead," I tell Mrs. C., when we're together, coming home from Katherine's, crossing the river in the near dark, passing the Weihnauchtsmarkt. "You go and I'll buy chocolate for dinner, Austrian strudel, bratwurst for all."

She is exhausted, and she goes. She puts her arms around me, hugs me, slips some euros in my pocket, and I think how Nadia will look exactly like her some day, hugging her best friend's daughter in an Italian market. Nadia will grow up to be just like Mrs. C. Nadia will grow up. Period.

I walk the Weihnauchtsmarkt by myself, looking for Benedetto. I check the crowds, I check the shadows. I spy, stealthy, into the windows all lit up around the piazza, checking for hair with a glow.

I'm looking for the boy Nadia needs.

I'm looking for the something she has lost. Not stolen.

Two weeks ago Katherine announced that it was my turn to design the week's intensive—constraint-induced therapy, in case I lost you on that. Force the mind to do what the mind has stopped doing. Re-grid, re-groove the neuronal pathways. Convert unused brain space into something bright and smart. Pump up the acetylcholine. Help Nadia lose the vague and sharpen the vocab, keep her mind alert and on guard. Attentive. Retentive. Old Nadia.

Think of a mash-up of Crazy Eights, Go Fish, and Charades. Think of a thirty-two-card deck, and sixteen images twice repeated. You start with four cards each and you're rooting for pairs. You have to ask, as specifically as you can: "Mrs. C., may I please have the spumoni card?" or "Do you have the tiramisu?" or "I need that picture of Lady Esquire, advertising leather shoe paint, 1974." If you can't express your wants explicitly, you express them as best as you can. If there's a chance to go all extemporaneous, do. You're not just dealing out nouns with this game. You're dealing memory and narrative continuity.

So it goes: "May I please have the card with the picture of pancetta? That's precisely what I want—the pancetta that reminds me of Marcella that reminds me of parsley, which is maybe a spice, maybe an herb. May I please have that?"

Then: "May I please have the picture of the mohair hot pants? Good God, I remember those mohair hot pants; every girl at Penn had a pair. We wore them in September, we wore them in October, and I was wearing them still, on that day in November, when Frederick Hartt, my art history professor, showed up and said there'd been a flood. I was wearing hot pants that day; I remember. I never touched the things after that, that's the truth. But still, right now, I would love the hot pants card, Nadia, if you happen to have it."

Until: "Maggie, may I, Maggie, I would like the pic—ture of, you know, when we ate, at Manake—, and after we bought Second—, and you said, you said, I said, So you'll remem—me."

"The *labneh!*" I'll answer. "The super-fresh, super-fine *labneh.* The yogurt cheese of Manakeesh. And you're right, I bought you your sweater that day? The one you're wearing, and it worked, because look. Here I am and here you are. Nobody forgetting nobody in Florence."

We give each other the cards when we have them. We hope Nadia will win, every time.

The intensives are incremental. They are relevant. They are specific. With every word Nadia wrestles back, with every advance in fluidity, we make it harder, up the ante, give her more of herself back. Week one was the food intensive: rigatoni, gnocchi, gemelli, pappardelle; spumoni, cannoli, panettone, tiramisu; *labneh*, shawarma, *kafta, tawook*. Week two (thank you, Mrs. C.) we focused on fashion: midi skirts, hot pants, skinny jeans, bell bottoms; mohair, rhinestones, leather, suede; platforms, Mary Janes, wedges, slingbacks.

Week three is now, and it is my turn, and I drew every one of the sixteen pictures with a couple of Vitale gel pens, then multiplied the force by two at the copying machines at the *biblioteca*, then trimmed and slicked each card with glue, to give it all a steady shellac.

"What do we have?" Katherine asks on this Monday, when we arrive, the little girl in her red sweater and cowboy boots back in her house. *Ciao. Ciao.* I say, "What we have here is architecture, good and simple. We have the places we have been." I spread my cards out on Katherine's kitchen table for all of us to see—Nadia, Katherine, Mrs. C., and me. We all take a good long steady look. Katherine sips tea. Mrs. C. smiles.

"Let us begin," Katherine says, tipping an egg timer, and I go first. "Nadia, do you have a picture of Manakeesh, where we eat the fine *labneh?*"

"Manak—eesh," she says, handing me the card. "Manakeesh." No air between the sounds.

"Maggie," Katherine says. "Do you have a picture of Second Mile Style, where apparently you buy all your fabulous things, and which I will surely visit as soon as I return to the city of Brotherly Love?"

"I am Second Mile Style," I say. Standing up. Twirling my high-low fashion. Then slapping a card down.

"Do you have a picture of San Miniato, that little church on the top of the hill?"

"I do," Mrs. C. says. "Absolutely."

We go three rounds. We get in good stuff. My cards are really working—Florence and Philadelphia. Sister cities, after all. Maybe more than a strand of shared DNA. We go around asking questions, go around telling stories, go around with our fatter book of nouns. And now it's Nadia's turn, and she's asking me a question, she's laying her last card down, and it's the Basilica of Santa Croce, the sketch I'm proudest of. She puts it right down, faceup, on the table between us, and she looks at me, steady, in the eyes, and says:

"Maggie, may I   pleasehave—Bene—det—Benedet—"

"You want Benedetto," I say quietly.

"Yes," she says.

"A friend?"

She nods.

"Tell me where to find him."

She points to the card.

"Benedetto is in Santa Croce," I say, wanting to be very sure.

"Yes."

"In the church? In the piazza? In the neighborhood?"

She touches the card, hard, three times. Fierce, almost, almost so fierce that Katherine places her hand over Nadia's, calms her, watches.

"Are you sure?" Katherine says. "Are you sure this won't upset you?"

Nadia shakes her head. No. Yes.

Katherine looks at me. "Can you?"

"Benedetto," Nadia says. And she begins to cry.

"I will find him," I say. "I promise."

I look for the boy. I look everywhere. This thing I can do, this hero I can be, for my best friend. In the shadows, by the church, in the pews, at the feet of Dante. I am searching everywhere.

In the meantime, I have not come close to completing the business of returning the stolen stuff to its proper casings, tier four. I have, for example, the problem of that watch—a Timex military, as it turns out, plastic, black, disposable, circa 1982. A rare species of time, in the country of unceasing bell-chime time. *Where in the world of sauce and pasta did you get this thing,* I've wanted to ask Nadia, several times. But Katherine says that reminding Nadia of the steal will just lava-melt the guilt in her—throw her off the rails and all the way back to who she hopes not to become.

So I go along, hunting the match-to-match—up and down the alleys, in and out of shops, rummaging the old-and-new and the watch-repair fronts and the stores in which you can't really tell, from the sign and the interior darkness, what in fact they sell. I wear the watch on my wrist like a jailer's cuff. I hide it inside my gingham check or my seersucker sleeve and, of course, my coat royale with the frogs for buttons. I have traded out my patent-leather boots with the buckles for a pair of three-inch painted clogs, easier on the feet, which have gained a half size, thanks to the blisters. When I think I'm close to a match, I'll take the shop-keeper aside and ask for the scoop on their recent watch collection, making like I'm in the mood to buy.

"Ever get one of those weird Timexes in, military style, 1982?" I'll ask, using my Italian dictionary or a little of Perdita's help. When all I get is a shaken head, I tuck my chin, say I'm sorry, and move on. Return to the Vitales' with my watch arm feeling longer than my regular arm—like the weight of time itself has stretched it thin. The double hems on my coat royale have turned the color of rain.

Sometimes Perdita comes along with me, and it's fine because we talk about Jack, or because we talk about spicing, or because we talk about style, or because we both get that just walking side by side is a trusted form of friendship. Perdita comes to help with the Italian and she comes to help with the alleys and how they bend and how the storefronts tuck in, and I never go too far with Perdita out there, because she always knows when to turn back.

"It's spicer knowledge," she tells me. "Like how you know pre-cisely how much chili pepper you can add before a dish goes from dancing to crashing." I let the theory slide. If we're done already for the day, we'll grab an early lunch at Sant'Ambrogio—the stall in the back, where they slap some sweet cream cheese onto the bread with a spatula knife and then lay out a line of proscuitto. We'll get chocolate later at the Bianchini bottega: mango-coriander-ginger for us, passionfruit with szechuan pepper for Jack, back at the apartment, working the Brunelleschi paper now like it's a doctoral thesis. Like Nadia's life depends on it.

"The crazy genius of the guy," Jack will say.

And we'll know what he means.

But this morning it wasn't Perdita who wanted to head out on the match-to-match. This morning I was slurping through my second cup of the prof's hot-milk specialty when he asked if he could come along and help with the unstealing project, and with the boy Nadia's desperate to find.

"You want to . . . help?" I asked.

He nodded.

"Could be futile," I said, and he said, "I am my daughter's father." And that, I agreed, is quite enough, and then he said, "This is my fault. All this. I was too flood-obsessed to see what was happening in real time."

"Don't be stupid," I said, as respectfully as I was able. "It's a disease," I said, "hurtled down the tracks. You don't trust me? Ask Dr. Roy. 'Disease is never anybody's fault,' he says. 'Blame abnormal proteins,' he says. 'Blame loss of neurons. Blame scar tissue in the brain.' Blame not yourself, and don't blame Nadia."

"I'm her father," the prof said. *I'm her father,* and I said, "I'd be privileged to have your help, Prof," and he thanked me, like it was a gift I'd given. He gathered his hat and coat, neither one (in case you're wondering) high on any particular style. I grabbed the Timex and my coat royale. I waited as he kissed Mrs. C. I waited as he roughed up Jack's thatchy hair, threw the Skullcandies out of alignment.

"Yo," Jack said.

"Tell Katherine and Nadia I'll be there closer to ten," the prof said, because that's how the days are divided here—Jack and the prof on the hill in the morning, me and Mrs. C. in the afternoon.

"Start it without you?" Jack asked. The music that had been pounding in his ear now pounding in the flat.

"I won't be that late."

Jack hitched the tune back onto his ears, said goodbye, and we were off.

Out the door and through the vestibule and farther out. The across-the-street neighbor had hung her clothes on a line outside her window, and the underwear was stiff, and the prof looked up and shook his head. "Funny to live in a city where you know the size of people's shorts but never the people," he said. Then he fixed the hat on his head, blew heat onto his hands, and asked me where we were going, and I told him my plans.

I'd had a thought about the neighborhood east of the *biblioteca.* I'd thought that we should go down Verrazzano and through the German market and past the Santa Croce gates, the cloisters, and around the library and out onto the Lungarno and then cut back in toward the poorest streets of all of Santa Croce, where there are a few shops, according to Perdita, and maybe, just maybe, a boy. Two birds. One stone. The prof agreed. We walked and together scanned the shadows. Nothing. A few birds high up, a few close, but no more. When we got to the Lungarno, he crossed over and stopped. Stood in the raw weather and stared into the face of the Arno. I crossed with him, stood there too, asked him what he was looking for, said I doubted the boy was down there.

"The river's a trickster," he said. And then he asked, "What are our chances?" And then he said, "What I don't get is why the kid himself hasn't come back. If he exists. If he is real. What are our chances?"

I thought you could take the question to mean anything. What are our chances at unstealing the Timex? What are our chances at finding the boy? What are our chances at saving Nadia? What are our chances of ever actually knowing when any story begins? What are our chances of figuring out how a story like this one might end?

What are our chances?

I thought on it. I watched the smokers down on the dam and the seagulls that peck around like pigeons, and a great heron lifting off from the banks near the Ponte Vecchio. I watched our own reflections in the flat, mealy river—the prof in his white hair and me in my red hair, blowing over the shoulders of my coat. I said chance is what we make of it, that's all I knew, and he said, if only that were so, if only we could make more of the chances we had. If only we could make more chance itself.

"It's all how you see it," I said.

"What do you mean?" he asked.

"Well," I said, "take Azelide, the old lady the river killed fifty years ago."

"What about Azelide?"

I told him what I'd been told by Jack and Perdita one day when we were stuck in the house because of the rain and we were watching it slide down the windows. Perdita told the story. She told it sad and well. It's a family story, she said, and it was hard to picture because I've never seen the girl's family. But she talked.

Azelide was, I repeat back to the prof, a lady sixty-six years old with numb legs and a wheelchair. She lived on the ground floor of an apartment building behind the Santa Croce basilica. Her apartment was grilled in, in defense against thieves, and on the day of the flood her apartment, being low in a low place, was one of the first to start drowning. By the middle of that November day everything Azelide owned was in a float—the bread, the flower-pots, the couch, the books. She cried for help, and help came—the priests and the nuns. They came, and they stood in the street trying to break down the door, trying to yank the window grilles out, but poor Azelide was barricaded in and all they could do was tie a sheet to her wheelchair and knot the sheet around the window grille and pass the sheet back through the window into the street, and to stand there, holding the sheet that was holding Azelide up, above the water. In the terrible rain, on this terrible day, the priests and the nuns stood outside Azelide's window and held onto that sheet until the water rose above their own chins. And then, when they could not stand there any longer, they said a prayer for Azelide.

"It's a very sad story," the prof said. "It's tragic."

And yet, I say, it was the best chance taken. Love. Faith. Hope. They stayed with Azelide until the end. They did everything they could.

Every.

Single.

The prof scratched a place behind his ear and ground his jaw-bones so I could see them working, like an animal inside his skin. He stared down into the mirror of the river and into the mirror of my eyes and shook his head. Yes and no and yes again.

"Love. Faith. Hope," he said. "The best chance taken."

"Yeah."

The trickle of the river was running. The cars of the Lungarno were going past. The big windows of the *biblioteca* looked down on us from across the street.

"How old are you, Maggie?" he asked.

"Same age as Nadia. Seventeen."

"To going the distance," he said.

We stood there for a while, let the wind blow. We watched a seagull fight the breeze to land on the barren concrete of the dam, where a lone fisherman now stood, looking for action. It would rain soon, but snow would not be coming, and the Christmas red that lit the belly of the bridges was still Florence-style festive.

"We have work to do," I told him, and we started off again, east, before cutting into a side street, north. Pulling our coats close against our chests.

Now in the small streets of Santa Croce we walk the cobbled stones. There are three girls, arm in arm, singing some Italian song. There are cats on the stoops and in the flower boxes. There's a wicker basket on a bike, piled high with onions, and I wonder what kind of stew is in store for that family, wonder how that house will smell for days afterward. We walk looking for a special boy, taking our chances. Walk in advance of the match-to-match, the Timex beating out the seconds on my wrist.

The houses are crooked and stuccoed, lopsided or square. The street curves around like a kitten chasing its tail, except for the one house that is different from the rest, its face painted blue, its trim painted the color of a warm cherry pie, maybe a cranberry pie, definitely pie. The people who pass keep their chins tucked in, their hands in their pockets, no flowers, no flames. The prof keeps pressing his eyebrows back, as if that will help turn on some superpower vision.

We don't find a boy with illuminated hair, but we do find a shop, our feet already wet and the hem on my coat the color of coal. The shop is a hole in the wall—a cave of plaster heads and cornices, fireplace mantels and jewelry boxes, rings for gnarly fingers, old door handles and milk jugs, silverware and ironed-over tablecloths. Not antiques, exactly, and not thrift. Only everything that was.

"You think she was here?" the prof asks, when we stop at the door. I tell him nothing can be known for sure, but still, this is a chance, and so he takes off his hat, like he's stepped foot into church, and he lets me do my business as I do my business now, asking the question about the Timex '82. Ever seen one of them? Ever *sell* one?

The shopkeeper closes his eyes and rocks on his heels, regal and medieval, like a character from *Game of Thrones,* with no hair, Italian shoes, and a grandmother's apron. He says he thinks maybe he remembers a watch like that, how he noticed it because of how strange it was, how they only ever built that watch for two months in that one year of 1982. "I might have seen that watch," the shop-keeper says, in Italian, closing his eyes and trying to remember, and I stare at him hard to see whether he looks like someone who has been taken from, whether Nadia was here after all. It's a tough call. It's not clear. I'm on my own—the prof retreated to the back of the shop, to the books and magazines, stained as tea. I make the decision on my own: Nadia's Timex is staying with me.

"Thank you," I tell the guy in the shop. "Prof," I say, and as soon as I say his name, he looks up and startles—not at me, but something beyond me, through the window of the shop.

"What is it?" I ask as we hurry out the door.

"I thought I saw," he says. "I thought . . ."

"What?"

"Someone running."

But there is nothing but three girls singing in the Santa Croce streets, walking down the cobbled stones with their arms like daisy chains.

When I get back to the Vitales' on Verrazzano, Agnese is in the vestibule pacing, smoking her cigarette, calming her puppy. The prof is on his way up the hills. I'm alone with the watch on my Gumby wrist, alone with the chance we might have had, or maybe it was just the weird mist-light of Florence.

"He was just here," Agnese says, in her Italian American as soon as she sees me, her dog on alert.

"Who was?"

"The boy you were asking for. The boy with the hair." She kisses the part of her dog that fluffs up between his ears. His pink tongue falls out, like bubblegum taffy. He yips.

I take a *whoa* step back, settle my heart flutter, take a breath.

"Benedetto?"

"*Si.*"

"Did he knock? Did you . . ."

"No. He was down there. Looking up. I wasn't dressed, and then I got dressed, and by the time I got down to the street, he was gone."

"You're sure?"

"Hair like light?" she says. "Hair that glows?"

I look at her face, her beautiful Italian face, and I know she is telling the truth. That she is trying to help us, like she is always trying to help us, playing music to appease us, keeping an eye out.

"Which way?"

She stomps through the vestibule in her high, open-toed heels. She presses the latch, pulls on the door, opens us up to the weather, points south toward the piazza. The dog yips. The cigarette's finished. She stomps it to a smolder.

"Agnese," I say, "thank you." Throwing my arms around her quick. I take off at a clip, bunching my coat up with my fists. I reach the end of Verrazzano in no time, cut through the German market, between the red-and-white awnings, past the oompah band. Far away, near the four fierce lions at the base of the Dante-with-his-cap-on statue, I see what I would describe to you as supernatural color.

I see it. I swear.

I take off even faster now—eyes on the prize, painted clogs hard on the cobbles, hem dragging, who cares. I swing in and out of the morning shoppers until bam, bang, I'm stopped dead cold by a mother pushing a baby in a wicker carriage.

"Excuse me," I say. "Sorry!" Looking down at the baby and up at the mother and hoping they'll push out of the way. They don't. The wheel of the carriage is stuck on the paving and for a moment we are hanging there, like a freeze-frame in a film, all three, until I jiggle the carriage free. I'm thanked, but I'm no hero. There was a chance, but I lost it. At Dante's base only the lions sit and the eagle flaps its stone wings.

"Jesus," I say, and the chimes go off, and I check the stolen Timex: noon.

I have an hour, still, to look around. I buy a ticket to the cathedral.

Not like I haven't been here before. I've sat in the pews beside Mrs. C. staring up at the scaffolding and staring back into the Franciscan space, talking about Nadia and at-risks and big faith and not giving in to giving in. I've counted the tight arches and I've Our Father'ed before the tombs that are like houses. I've guarded the vapors of Michelangelo and Galileo and whatever else survives the genius soul. The paint on the frescoes in the sixteen chapels is the color of faded velvet in the windows of old homes, and it's bigger than a soccer field in here. Bigger than any Ivy League graduation. So big, so too easily big, to choose to hide in shadows.

Take a chance, Benedetto. Show yourself.

It is not a busy day in the cathedral. Only small knots of people are here or there, before the Giotto, before the sacristy, before the redheaded Madonna, in the postcard store. I hear the church bell ring and check the Timex, and it is one o'clock. I take another tour through, remember the *Lonely Planet* caution box—the sidebar on Stendhal syndrome, also called hyperkulturania. Basic story, in a nutshell: Stendhal, the French guy, came in here and saw so much beauty that he got sick.

Too much beauty can make you sick.

Show yourself, I think.

Show yourself, Benedetto.

Mrs. C. has already left for the hill. I call for her at the flat when I get back, but she's gone, and I change my shoes and comb my hair—pile it up away from my face and nail the bun in with a gel pen. If Agnese is home, she's not playing the piano, and Jack and the prof are at lunch, the way they do after their own intensives on the hill. It's just me and the ghosts of the Vitales, looking out on Verrazzano, so I lock the door behind me and leave the flat, get on my way toward my best friend on the hill.

Down again, through again, over. Three kids grabbing a smoke on the concrete beach of the dam, the fisherman gone. Belvedere seems far today, too high up and tucked away, and when I stop to catch my breath I look back east, over my shoulder, toward San Miniato, like a toy in Legoland. A boy so fast even God couldn't catch him. A boy maybe in the backstreets of Santa Croce. A boy maybe at Verrazzano.

Find him.

When I turn back around I see the little girl in the red sweater and cowboy boots. She's farther down the hill than usual, looking concerned until she sees me. She raises one hand and waves, then raises the other to advertise a new doll, floppy and soft, and suddenly I'm filled with lonesomeness for the girl I used to be, the girl Nadia used to be. Girls who didn't know how scary and random and upside down life can turn out to be.

"*Buon Natale!*" she calls, and as I rise higher and higher up the hill, I see how the box of her house is lit from within by a bulbed evergreen. The girl blows me a kiss and turns on her heel, her skirt kicking up behind her and the lights in her house blinking on and off. Almost Christmas. She's wanting me to know, thinking I'd forgotten.

In Katherine's house they're already at the table with a tin of cookies and three mugs of tea. I leave my coat on, the cold air caught in my hair; I shiver. Katherine stands to reach the kettle on the stove and Nadia stands too, steps forward, hugs me hard, says hello. Lights in the wells of her eyes, asking the question:

"Have you?"

"Still looking."

"We have some news," Mrs. C. says, interrupting. She has her red turtleneck on, her black yoga pants, her hair in a simple ponytail, her reading glasses halfway down her nose and the news she has is, I can tell, far more important than the news I can't deliver.

"What is it?"

"We got a call from California."

"Let Nadia tell," Katherine says.

I turn, look at my best friend again, the light in her eyes changing, a slow smile on her face, a sad slow smile. She steps back, gathers her words, puts them all together in her head before she speaks them out loud.

"Dr. Bruce," she begins. "Dr.—Bruce. The clin—ic. Clinical-trialopening." The last words spilling in a crystallizing rush.

"When?"

"Just after Christmas," Mrs. C. says, standing up now, hands on her hips, her arms out like the slight wings of a Cornish hen.

She has already made plans, I can tell. Already scheduled the trip in her head, put Jack back into the school in Philly, the prof back onto the campus at Penn, Nadia and herself in a sublet in the rusty hills of San Francisco, for a month, maybe two months, maybe three months, I don't know, until Nadia's progress can be monitored somewhere closer to home. The clinical trial is opening. The clinical trial for the pharma intensive that may bring Nadia closer to whole.

I think of the world outside—the Christmas market, the Duomo tree, the dendrite lights, little Sophia Loren and her early Christmas present. Christmas is soon. Christmas and hope, maybe, a cure, possibly, a fix for the at-risk, good news. A chance presented, a chance taken. But also: If Nadia leaves before she sees Benedetto, something I don't understand will be ruined. Lost.

"Nadia," I say. "Sweetie. I'm so glad."

She hugs me again, harder, her scabby hand healed by now and her hair long to her waist and her bare feet pale on the planks of Katherine's floor. She hugs me and stands back and looks at me with her sad-happy eyes, and then at Katherine, complicated Katherine, standing by the stove with the kettle in her hand, her hair pulled over one shoulder. When Nadia leaves, Katherine will stay. She will lose us. Every day. Alone in the hills of Belvedere.

"We need to be cautious," Katherine says. "With our hope."

"Of course."

"We need to take one day at a time."

"Yes," Mrs. C. says.

Though Christmas is soon.

"Let's keep to our routine for this day at least," Katherine says, and now she steps forward with my mug of tea in her hands. I bring the steam to my face as she slips the deck of my cards from the pile of *Brain* magazines, tall as a column. She shuffles twice, hands the deck to me, and I place my mug on the table, reshuffle the deck, deal, sit down. I unfrog the buttons on my coat and wait for Nadia to pull out her chair, to pick up the cards, to scan her two sister cities—Florence and Philadelphia. She studies her hand hard, rearranges things. She looks up when she is ready. I take in a long draught of tea and it runs down my throat, past my heart.

Mrs. C. starts. She asks for the bright-red face of the Fisher Library, and Nadia has this card, hands it over, an easy exchange. Katherine goes next, requests the Pitti Palace; I surrender it. I ask for the Woodlands and Mrs. C. makes it mine, and now it's Nadia's turn and everyone waits until she is ready to speak.

"Maggie," she starts, "can I have please I have, canIhave Frank—lin Field."

"All yours," I say, pinching the card to lay it down, but she puts her hand on my hand and stops me, pushes back, stands and walks to where I'm sitting and works her hands up into my hair. She slips the gel pen free and unknots the tangles. She smooths the strands, begins to braid, her fingers going *whisk whisk whisk*—one braid beside the other, six long zippers, and I think of all the times I braided her hair and how never once could I braid like this—so fast, so efficient, the weave of an artiste. Like being inside one of Nadia's nests, I think, and I wait for her to tell me what she wants.

She leans across my shoulder, slips a card out of my hand, lays it flat. Santa Croce.

"Gardenofleather," she says. "Findhim."

I have looked, I wanted to say. I have looked, I have run, I have followed Agnese's pointing finger. Agnese who lives her life in a cloud of smoke and a thrum of sad piano. Agnese who can't be certain, whom I can't be certain of. I have looked, Nadia, I am trying.

Maybe he's not real.

Maybe . . .

But I hug her. I say nothing. She is my best friend. She trusts me most. We are each other's miracle. World's greatest.

I wake in the dark. So hard to sleep at the Vitales'. So hard to dream and not see Nadia. So hard to be alone, counting out chances.

Jack's in the other room, rustling in his bed. There's the *pop-pop* of the prof's snoring. There's Mrs. C. pulling a tea bag out of the canister she brought from the house in West Philadelphia, and as I wait the charcoal sky in the window grows pewter, and now a band of possible sun cuts through. I pull on my traffic-light dress with the triple flounces, circa 1970, and the Timex, 1982, which will never be unstolen, and the coat, its hem frayed.

I open the window, let in the cold air. I think of last winter, when the snow fell fast over Philadelphia and Nadia remembered the old coil of rope in the basement and the metal slick of the trash can lid and how she had said, "Climb on," and I did. And how we went all the way through West Philadelphia and all the way around the Quad, and how we could look in and see the students in their dorm rooms looking back at us, and how up ahead Nadia looked like a star. The light from the dorm was on her like a star. She had ice crystals in her hair and snow ridges on her shoulders and there were candles in her eyes and her skin was winter-colored. She looked like the angel she had carried home from Curiosities. She looked like she might fly away, except for the rope tied tight between us.

It is so cold out there in Florence. So cold and possibly wet; it could snow soon. In the glass room where the bookbinder works, a light snaps on, and I stay right where I am—in the cold front of the early day. He takes his seat on his tall stool with the wooden back. He sits at his long, crowded table. He stacks and unstacks his signatures, measures for holes, punches the holes, threads a needle, and I watch him work, his shirtsleeves rolled. His hands play at the work like piano keys. Ribbons flutter above his head. Ribbons: I've seen them before. I've seen—

Wait.

I've seen these ribbons.

Careful, I think.

Don't presume. Ask.

I watch him—very keen. I see how he reaches up to collect a tool, and when the cuff of his sleeve pulls away from his wrist I see a big clunky thing, a circa 1980s Timex, and that's how I know for insta-sure. Suddenly, brilliantly, hard-to-breathedly, I have our match-to-match.

The stolen from was there all along, in the back alley.

The thief lived in this room, watched from this window, could not help herself.

Look up, Mr. Bookbinder, I think.

Look up and see.

My best friend is an artiste, like you.

As soon as Mrs. C. slips back into her room, I slip out. Down the stairs, past the stink of bikes, into the cold, where I hear the sound of suds at the Laundromat. A waiter locks the door to his car, then carries a tray of lettuce in through the front door of the restaurant.

There is one small alley that leads into the back courtyard, and I follow the trail, hurrying now, my coat pulled to my chest, my pocket heavy. There is a wide sill beneath the binder's window. I stand on my toes. I reach the sill. I leave the Timex right there, a long-lost present. I leave it with a note.

WE'RE SORRY.
WE TOOK FOR BEAUTY'S SAKE.
WE MEANT NO HARM.
WE'RE GRATEFUL.

No one out on Verrazzano now but a Bolognese pup, doing his business near the foot of the scaffolding. Somebody whistles and the furball scampers across the street and out of sight and I'm alone again, the white band of sun turning a cream-in-coffee color.

The Timex has been restored.

The clinical trials are starting soon.

The days are running short.

Find him.

Across the piazza, Santa Croce looks like a kindergarten drawing. There's someone asleep on its steps—two students with boxes for guitars and backpacks for pillows. I stand at Dante's feet looking up, looking around, and then I look straight past him. There, along the north side of the basilica, the east end, is a door I've never noticed—the color of copper over time. An older man is fitting a key into its lock, jangling the handle. The door opens, and then it shuts. Another way into Santa Croce.

I study the creamed milk of the sky. I wait in the shadows, take my time. When I reach the door and pull, it gives. I hear footsteps far away, and then the footsteps vanish and I'm standing here, in a frame of light, watching Jesus die in the arms of his mother.

I follow a hallway down, long and wide, smooth as the inside of a tulip, plastered arches overhead until the surfaces begin to break and the plaster is brick and there are small rooms furnished with marble and light off to the one side. When the hallway juts right I stop. The sky is here. A winter garden. The December bark of olive trees and oranges in hibernation. *Garden of leather*, Nadia had said. But everything here is green or dreaming green. It's flora and not fauna.

I sit on the half wall, blow on my hands, wonder where Benedetto is hiding, if he is hiding, if he exists. A couple of brown birds, chickadees, maybe, have flown in from the sky above and are grubbing for crumbs on the stone floor, bobbing their heads, tweeting. One bird leaves the pack and hops up onto the last branch of the tree, then disappears, and now I see it again, higher. It hops again and I see how it leaves and returns, hunting.

"Can I help you?"

Startled, I turn and find not the man with the key but a woman with a summer tan and a fringe of white hair, her eyes so large and specific that it's clear she's been watching me watch the birds for a while in this open nest of weather.

"It's early," she says when I don't answer. "The basilica doesn't open for a few hours more. Nor the shops," she says. "Nothing. You shouldn't be here."

"I didn't realize," I say, and I stand to go, but she looks at me like she wants me to stay, or like we are not done. She wears a short, furry coat and a blue pencil skirt. Black shoes with blue heels. A large gold ring.

"I'll have to talk to Carlos," she says, "about the door."

Her English is perfect. Her eyes are so green. I think of chances. I ask her.

"I'm looking for someone," I say.

Her eyebrows arch up, the hoops in her ears glitter.

"*Oof.*" She shakes her head. "Young love."

"No," I say. "That's not what I mean. It's not for me. It's for a friend."

"A friend."

"Who isn't well. And there's this boy. Benedetto. Have you heard of him? She says he's here, at Santa Croce. *Garden of leather,* she said. So I came here. I've come here. I've looked everywhere. And now I'm here, and now I wonder: Is there even a boy named Benedetto?"

She gives me a long look and then a nod. She touches the elbow of my coat and turns and I follow her, around another corner, another courtyard, toward another opening to the sky.

The rooms are stone here; rustic, not smooth. The windows are long, and through them I see a world of tools and skins, dyes and knives, old-fashioned sewing machines, a little row of plastic men on the brick sill, big windows; the old man, Carlos. We step into his workshop, and I wait while she speaks to the man in Italian, fast, and I hear the boy's name, twice. Carlos looks up from what he has in his hands and he studies me with watchful eyes. He says a few words, just a few, and then they are done, and now she touches me again, and we step out of the workroom and beneath the sky, and she tells me her news, a quiet story.

"It's as I thought," she says. "The boy is still on leave. Something to do with his mother."

"So," I say, can barely say it, "there is a boy."

"Yes, of course," she blinks. "The boy we have been discussing."

"A real boy?"

"Is there some confusion?"

"Named Benedetto."

She doesn't smile. She doesn't nod. Her eyebrows furrow.

"Yes," she says at last. "*Si*."

"It's important that I find him," I say, my heart thumping. "It's—it's absolutely necessary. Can you tell me where he lives? Can you call him for me, please? Can you—oh my God," I plead. The words stuttering around like my best friend's words stutter around. Everything broken. Everything a miracle.

The woman stands there a long time, considering. She shakes her head, very slow. She says that I must understand that they cannot give private information out to strangers, that that is not what they do in her country.

I feel the tears in my eyes, try not to beg. I ask her, please, again, one more time, isn't there anything she can do, give me his number, his last name, anything—please. She shakes her head no. Asks if by chance my friend is the girl with the dark hair and the professor father.

"You know her?" I say.

"I met her," she says. "She was watching Benedetto work. She seemed—nervous, perhaps. Not well. Fragile," she decides. "That's what she seemed. Fragile." One word. Italian flares.

"Nadia Cara is my best friend," I say.

"Ah, yes. *Si*. I see."

"She needs me to find Benedetto. She needs to speak to him. Just tell me his last name. Please."

"You must understand," she says. "I cannot."

She runs a finger around the inside of one hoop, like running a finger around the thoughts in her head. She looks terribly sad, terribly perplexed, terribly concerned, but there are rules, proprieties.

"The boy carries a pink duffel bag," she tells me, quietly, finally. "Very bright pink. Drives a Vespa. Very old. If you look for both things, you will find him."

"I'm running out of time," I say.

"I am hoping for you," she says.

"But you—"

"No," she says. "I'm sorry."

"Here," I say, scribbling an address onto a scrap I find in my purse, scribblng a phone number over the address. "Call him. Tell him Nadia says hello. Tell him Nadia is leaving soon."

I step back and back and back, backward. She holds the paper in her hands. She lets me go.

Like walking through an empty subway station. Past the garden and the bird, past the empty rooms of worship, the diorama rooms, past Jesus still dying, and up, and out, to the Christmas streets of Florence.

Please, I said. *Please.*

There is no other more pitiable word.

Out under the sky I walk east and then north to the Sant'Ambrogia market. I file through the outside stalls of winter vegetables, climb the stairs, and wander under the bright lights, nothing supernatural here, no bright pink duffel, my heart down around my knees, my whole self sunken. I find the baker and order three panettone and wait while she wraps them in white boxes with blue ribbons. One for the Caras. One for Katherine. One for Nadia alone. *I didn't find him,* I'll have to say. *I almost found him,* I cannot say. This close. *This* close. But nothing.

Only a few days left until Christmas, and, after Christmas, San Francisco, an experimental intervention.

Hope.

I wanted to save you, Nadia. I wanted to be your best-friend heroine.

I wanted miracles.

I walk slowly toward the Vitales', the boxes in my hands. I let the bikes with the streamers and the finger-flicked bells pass. The two nuns with tube socks and baskets, their thick bike wheels fighting the grooves between cobbles. The two men carrying a chunk of an altar in their hands, their hands like stirrups. A woman in a terrycloth coat with the belt strings hanging down, like she got lost on her way to the shower. It is gray and gray-silver and gray-white out here, dirt in the stones of Florence, and I am not far from the Vitales' when I see it. Fluorescent as a traffic cone. Pink as a flamingo. The red tongues of a poinsetta in its mouth. The fumes of a Vespa.

"Wait," I call after it. "Stop!" The three boxes of panettone in my arms, and the bikes and the terrycloth amnesiac in my path, and me calling *Benedetto!* Following the trail of the smoke, the turn of the streets, the grooves of the cobbled stones. The boxes earthquake in my arms. The hem of my coat drags and catches on the curb, and he is getting away from me, I am losing him again, vanquishing chance. "Stop!" I call, and now the nuns with their bells see what I need, see how I am, and they decide: They pull up their skirts and ride their bikes harder and flick their fingers at their bells. They disappear where he disappeared. I call and everything is silent. Only the sound of my painted clogs echo across the cobbles.

The street has bent again, it has dodged left. I take the turns as they come, follow the smell of the Vespa, listen to my own sad painted clogs, until there, far away, I see him. The boy with the hair, on the bike, the pink duffel bag on his shoulder flying.

"Wait!" I call. "Wait! Wait!"

But he looks one way and then the other, and never once looks back, and now I think I am becoming Nadia, or I understand Nadia, or I can see inside her brain. Because what is a dream, and what is imagined, and what in this world is for real?

Actual real?

I am losing my way in the heart of Florence.

These streets are so confusing.

December 20, December 21, December 22, December 23.

The days go by, but the days are different. Suitcases in the hall. Mrs. C. on the phone, long-distance. The prof out in the early fog, walking the length of his river. Jack is near to the end of his Brunelleschi paper, and while he works, Perdita sits in the window making chains for the miniature tree that we rooted into a pot at the Vitales'. Upstairs Agnese plays Christmas songs like she is practicing for a concert, like she can help us. In the windows we've hung Chinese lanterns shaped like stars, and beneath the stars, on the sills, burn white candles. Between her calls and her arranging, Mrs. C. has pulled out all the Vitales' pots and made a pigeon sauce, and that was enough for Jack to set aside his paper and return to Almost Independent Study 101—to take out all the pots, to buy up all the spices, to cook, Perdita as his sous chef. In the closet in the hall, behind a coat made of bearskin, I found the Vitales' wooden crèche and it sits on the chest of drawers beside the TV.

In the mornings I walk the streets looking for Benedetto, hoping for another chance. In the afternoons, I go with Mrs. C. to the hill of Belvedere, and we talk nouns and play intensives, remember Christmas words. Mistletoe. Twinkle lights. Stocking stuffers. We sit warming our hands with mugs of tea and eating the raisins out of stollen.

"Ishecoming?" Nadia asks, as soon as I arrive.

"Not yet," I say. "Don't know."

I lost him.

I am my best friend's best friend. I am here. It rains too much in Florence. Katherine says I should know that I've done all I can.

Love. Faith. Hope.

Which best chance, taken?

I walk the streets, I run the streets, I call his name:

Benedetto.

December 24. Christmas Eve.

We've hidden the tier-fours that were never unstolen. We've fit the nests inside boxes we found empty in the bottom of the Vitales' closets, wrapped each one like a gift, stowed them away. We've made the Vitales' front room big enough—the couch pulled back, the chairs circled round, the tree pulled into the middle—and we've tucked a candle there behind the crèche. Jack has gone all-out crazy in the kitchen, and Perdita has helped, and Mrs. C., too, and sometimes she leaves her son and Perdita and walks across the room and stands so close to her prof, her long hair with the few new white streaks falling before them like a curtain. He fits his hand into the small of her back. She smooths his eyebrows down with a damp finger.

I've Skyped home. I've written cards. I've given instructions for my garden. *Go and visit it, please. Check on the fig tree and its straw.* I hear the echoes of my painted clogs in the streets. I feel the pull of the rain in the hem of my coat.

Faith. Love. Hope.

The terrible hurt of my infinite failure.

"They're here," the prof says, and we all leave wherever we are to see for ourselves. Upstairs, above us, Agnese's piano song stops playing. The little dog yips, and down in the street Nadia hears it and looks up and smiles. Katherine, behind her, waves both her hands, like the girl on the hill with the doll.

"Look," Mrs. C. says.

"My primo," the prof whispers, his voice choked in his throat.

Nadia wears a long white borrowed coat and my patent-leather boots and her hair is swept back in a messy bun, trailing Christmas ribbons. Nadia the artiste, I think.

"Hey, Nads. Hey. Merry Christmas. Hey."

"You look so so pretty," I say, and Jack says, "Yeah," and Perdita reaches up to fix one of the ribbons in Nadia's hair, every fingernail painted a different bright rad color.

"Merry Christmas," Nadia says. Her words soft and sticky as jam.

Mrs. C. bought everything for Christmas that the Sant'Ambrogio Market has to offer—every spice and sausage, every cake and pigeon bone, all the angel hairs of pasta, all the chocolate flavors, every bit of cheesecake with the bitter orange marmalade. My stomach feels like the round part of a question mark. Our eyes are on each other and on Nadia. Our thoughts are on now and on days from now, on who we were and who we're still becoming. Jack and Perdita are holding hands. Nadia sits between me and the prof. Mrs. C. and Katherine have no words for the gain or the loss.

I have no match-to-match for my best friend.

"Should we do the Secret Santa?" Mrs. C. asks. "We should do the Secret Santa," she answers herself.

We groan when we move. We hurt when we rise. We go wherever we have to go to find the secrets we've been keeping for each other, each of us taking care of the names we drew a week ago, when we were sure Nadia would come. Her first time leaving Katherine's place in all this time. Her first time strong enough.

We stand up, ease down, reveal our secrets, one by one. A miniature Duomo and three jars of extra-hot on the scale of hot chili peppers for Jack (courtesy of the prof). A sterling silver *David* for Katherine (courtesy of Mrs. C.). A new phone for Mrs. C. because of her at-risk work (courtesy of the prof). A gold chain, bicycle-heavy and perfectly punk, for Perdita (courtesy of me) and also (courtesy of me) rad cable-knit tights, dyed lime green. Jack A-plussed his Brunelleschi paper—put math in it, history, a little neuro commentary on the wonders and the risks of genius, a Florence soundtrack. He put his whole heart in, and he loves Perdita, his bitter chocolate, his inch of punk.

Now, in Philly, Jack'll have his Miss Florence list, and there's nothing we can do about it, nothing he can say when Perdita slips her hand into her pocket and places a mini padlock onto his palm, like the kind that grows wild on the Ponte Vecchio, like the kind that says *Love you forever.* "Jesus, Perdita," Jack says, and he looks away, then looks straight at her, and now Mrs. C. gets up and says we have a special presentation, and she disappears down the hall and takes her time and comes back holding a Liberty print dress in one hand, a Jean Muir special, circa 1970. She holds a pretty beret in her other hand, its band trimmed in leather the color of dark honey.

"For our Miss Maggie Ercolani," Mrs. C. says, "who came and gave her all."

I get all choked up, can't talk. Nadia pulls her chair close and takes my hand in hers and one by one opens my fingers, and there, in the nest of my palm, places a folded photograph, like an origami bird. "Open," she says, and when I do I find the two of us looking back at me—a selfie taken the night we came back from riding the snow of Philadelphia.

"Thank you," she says. "Thank—you."

"I have something for you, too," I say, and from beneath my chair I slide a wrapped rectangle, Nadia's name written on the tissue in gel pen. She sits for a moment, then slides her finger through the seam of the tissue paper, breaking the Scotch-tape seals. She does it with an expert hand.

"What is it?" Jack asks, from across the room.

"Sister cities," I say, lifting the frame to show him how I've arranged the originals of the cards I drew, side by side, the architecture intensives.

"No," Nadia says, shaking her head. "Just sisters, Mag. Just— sisters."

"You and me," I say. "Forever. World's greatest miracle."

We sit with our gifts in our laps. We sit remembering. We sit holding on to right now because we cannot know tomorrow or the next day—the trials in San Francisco, the mystery magic of the brain. The prof stands and disappears down the hall and returns with a book, its cover built of Florentine papers, its belly wrapped in ribbon. A perfect bookbinder book.

"One of a kind," he says, pressing his eyebrows down and holding the little book up, cracking its spine. He stands there and clears his throat. Looks down and starts to read.

"'*Where the story begins*,'" he says.

He looks up at Mrs. C., then over to Katherine. He looks at Jack and Perdita and for a long time at Nadia, then turns another page and reads: "'*And how the rains fell. And how the River Arno rose and how this cinnamon city vanished. Down the channel of the streets and into the cellars of Santa Croce and between the bindings of books, the running muddy waters. Crucifixes. Paradise. Lady Magdalene. How the rains fell.*'"

He pauses. Turns another page. The paper cracks. The glue.

"'*But even that is not where our story begins. Our story begins, every story finally begins, with the possibility of rescue, with the goodness that is absolute and waits for tragedy to find it. Mud Angels,*'" the prof reads. "'*Dirty boots and redheaded birds. That's where the story begins. Always.*'"

"You found your beginning," Mrs. C. says, softly.

"No," he says, looking at Nadia. "We did."

All the things lost and all the things gained, that's what I'm thinking. All of us quiet here, turning the gifts in our hands, the memories we keep, the words we use to keep them, the hope we have, the work we do, our lives rearranging themselves. Time goes by. Nothing lasts. The bells in the towers of Florence sing. Every bell in every tower, clanging on and on.

"Midnight," Katherine says. A Christmas Eve tradition.

Nadia turns toward the window and stands. She cuts through the chair circle and past the crèche and stops beneath the Chinese lantern and the flames still burning on the sill. She fits her hand onto the window latch and presses down and pushes out and leans into the Christmas weather.

"Snow," she says. When we reach her side, when we stand there looking out it's birds we see—white birds with bright wings flying out of the towers, flying low and bright, the egrets of Florence. A half a moon and only a little rain, and bells and wings and bells.

But then:

"Bene—detto," Nadia says, almost cries. She says it again, leans so far out into the sky that we must hold her here with us. *Don't fall.*

"Shhhh," I say.

But she points, she grabs my hand, she points again, and now I follow her gaze down the narrow channel of Verrazzano. Down the cobbled street, beneath the dripping laundry, in between the start of snow.

It's the boy with the pink duffel, ripped to full with flowers.

The boy and sonic blooms.

ONE THING HOPED FOR

The rain has been plenty all winter. The rain and sometimes the snow.

White flakes.

Drift.

The faces of the flowers press down like showerheads. The band of leather pockets that I made in the shop brim with the start of things—oregano, parsley, basil, dill, thyme, marjoram.

Skinny.

Green.

Alive.

"Sit with me," Mama says.

Mama's eyes on the new shoots and the old flowers. Mama's eyes on the nests that I strung, one after the other, among the husks of stolen flowers, on the ledges of the limbs, in the hollow places of the plaster. Broken springs and half globes. Silk and string. Round and twig.

She wants you to have them, Maggie said, the week after Christmas, when she came all the way through the minor streets of Santa Croce, pulling a big sled behind her, a sled full of the beautiful and the strange. Carlos gave her the sled. Carlos called me in time. Carlos is our hero.

Nadia wants you to . . .

. . . have these, she said.

"*Guardare,*" Mama says now.

The nests like Christmas globes. The nests like so many perfect homes.

The news comes. Jack to Perdita to me. San Francisco to Maggie to me. Mrs. C. to Katherine to me. The news comes. I write back to whomever writes to me.

Tell Nadia that I'm waiting.

Tell Nadia that her nests are safe.

Tell Nadia that I understand.

Mama lies in her bed in the upside, in the down. She lies there and the seeds in the leather belt split some more and the sprouts wave their hands and the breeze through the window blows through the weaves of the nests, and the nests are so strong; the nests hold.

"So you're a genius," I said. Christmas Eve, just after midnight. "A genius. A bird girl. A thief."

"I am," she said. "Sorry."

"I am," she said. "Coming—back."

"Please donotforgetme."

I steal fresh flowers from the crypt, from the wedding shop, from the stalls of Sant'Ambrogio. I steal them out of window boxes and corner stores and baskets. I steal them and bring them here and hang them upside down, weave them alongside the nests, and every day, every single day, I think of Nadia, the genius of her, the courage in her, the nests she made to keep herself whole, to keep her bound to this one earth. When spring comes I will go out and find her birds—the egrets and the turtledoves, the green woodpeckers. I will tell them the news, tell them what has to be true, tell them the size and shape of hope, my one confession:

Nadia is coming back.

Not long now, not soon enough.

It rains until the sun comes out.

NOTES AND ACKNOWLEDGMENTS

The flood that raged through Florence in November 1966 did not just threaten an entire city; it sent ruinous mud and waters into the world's great museums and libraries; devastated an estimated four million historic books and manuscripts; saturated 14,000 works of movable art; destroyed the homes of 5,000 families; and pushed thousands of stores out of business. At the same time it gave birth to an international corps of bighearted volunteers who would be known forevermore as the Mud Angels. These were young people, mostly, who had faith that a broken world could be restored. These were the faces of hope. That faith and hope inspired me deeply as I wrote the book that would become *One Thing Stolen*.

I was first introduced to the floods of Florence through the magnificent book *Dark Water* by Robert Clark. It filled me with the desire to study a city I had loved in passing years ago, and taught me about beginnings, Cimabue, Azelide, and many other things. Three additional books—Swietlan Nicholas Kraczyna's *The Great Flood of Florence, 1966: A Photographic Essay*; Howard Greenfield's *The Waters of November*; and Katherine Kressmann Taylor's *Diary of Florence in Flood*—helped me see the Florence of the flood with greater clarity.

But to get to the heart of the flood, I traveled to Florence itself and sought out the survivors, the storytellers. I am particularly grateful to Emily Rosner and Maurizio Panichi, proprietors of the Paperback Exchange, just off the Piazza del Duomo, for sharing their stories and for working through Italian phrases with me. I am grateful to the shopkeepers who answered questions I asked and to Agnese, who rented my husband and me her apartment off Verrazzano, near the Santa Croce piazza. Their stories are part of this story, part of the great obsession. Thank you, as well, to Mario Sulit, my talented brother-in-law, whose great facility with so many languages helped me tremendously here.

I have been taught the art of nests and birds by a number of authors: Sharon Beals (*Nests*); Tim Birkhead (*Bird Sense and The Wisdom of Birds*); Peter Goodfellow (*Avian Architecture*); Thor Hanson (*Feathers*); Joy M. Kiser (*America's Other Audubon*); Rosamond Purcell, Linnea Hall, and Rene Corado (*Egg & Nest*); and Katrina van Grouw (*The Unfeathered Bird*).

I first came upon the rare brain disease known as frontotemporal disorder in a *New York Times* article by Sandra Blakeslee. In a story entitled "A Disease That Allowed Torrents of Creativity," Blakeslee wrote of the Canadian scientist Anne Adams and her sudden obsessive turn toward art—an obsession later traced to an inexorable decline in her frontal brain area—and a corresponding strengthening of the posterior regions. Bruce Miller, Anh Truong, Indre Viskontas, and Marie Foregeard—scientists on the vanguard—all took the time to answer questions that my student, Alice Ma, asked. I am grateful for their time, and for their interest. I am particularly grateful to Dr. Miller and the work he does as the director of the University of California, San Francisco Memory and Aging Center, where he advances the understanding of this disease. More about Dr. Miller's work can be found here: www.youtube.com/user/UCSFMemoryandAging.

One Thing Stolen is, of course, a work of fiction. I created Nadia to try to understand how such a condition might affect a person so young and to explore the power of neuroplasticity. Several books, including *Phantoms in the Brain* (V. S. Ramachandran, MD, PhD, and Sandra Blakeslee), *The Brain That Changes Itself: Stories of Personal Triumph from the Frontiers of Brain Science* (Norman Doidge, MD), and *The Tell-Tale Brain: A Neuroscientist's Quest for What Makes Us Human* (V. S. Ramachandran) helped deepen my understanding of emerging brain science.

Thank you to Greg Djanikian of the University of Pennsylvania for trusting me to teach on the campus of my youth, and who changed the trajectory of my career. Thank you to my students for being continuing sources of inspiration—Stephanie Cara, the world traveler, who lends Nadia her spectacular last name; Katherine Goldrath—Katie—whose big heart as a doctor-in-training is exemplary; Maggie Ercolani, who, at the age of just twenty, endured and with great grace recovered from an unexpected intercession.

Thank you to Kathryn Coffey, who sent me a copy of *Firenze su Misura* just in the nick of time, inspiring the character of the bookbinder. Thank you to Mike Cola, a true renaissance man, who saved, for me, the nests of birds, and who listened to me talk when this book was in its earliest stages. Thank you to Lori Waselchuk, the documentary photographer, for introducing me to the true West Philadelphia, Second Mile, Manakeesh, and Fiume. Thank you to Laura Gori, the gorgeous director of the Scuola del Cuoio, and to Carlos, who taught me how to bind the pages of a story together. Thank you to Wendy Robards, for asking, for caring, for waiting. Thank you, Ruta Sepetys, Patricia McCormick, and Debbie Levy for the work, the words, the friendship. Thank you, A. S. King, for sharing the adventure. Thank you to Kelly Simmons for the honesty and the ongoing conversation. Thank you, Jennifer M. Brown, for the glorious lunch on the day this story was finally done. Thank you, Amy Rennert.

Thank you, always, to Alyson Hagy. I can't imagine this writing life without you.

Thank you, Bill and Jeremy, for being real, and for making my life so rich.

Thank you to Debbie DeFord-Minerva, the copy editor who sent words of encouragement at precisely the right hour and soon became a friend. Thank you to Diane João, who patiently studied every space and dash and word.

Thank you to the entire Chronicle team—Ginee Seo, Lara Starr, Sally Kim, Stephanie Wong, Jaime Wong, Anna-Lisa Sandstrum, Taylor Norman, Johan Almqvist, Jenifer Savasta, Joya Anthony, Claire Fletcher, and Marie Oishi. I am so lucky to have found myself with all of you, and I feel blessed, daily, to be in the company of such a bold, imaginative, and generous team. Deep thanks to Kristine Brogno, who read the novel with care, slipped inside its physical and psychological landscape, and created a cover of rare ingenuity.

And thank you, finally and most especially, to Tamra Tuller, who waited patiently for this book to become the book it needed to be. There were detours, heaven knows. There were doubts—plenty. You were always there, by the side of the road, holding your lantern for me.

BOOK CLUB DISCUSSION GUIDE

1. Trace the nest and birds imagery throughout the novel. Discuss what they symbolize and what Kephart is able to accomplish through the use of these symbols.

2. Keep a list of the items that Nadia steals. What, if anything, is the connection between these items? What compels Nadia to steal them? Have you ever stolen anything, and if so, what and why? Do you believe that all things stolen should be returned to their original owners? Why or why not? What is your opinion in Nadia's case?

3. Think about the purpose of the secondary characters in the novel: Mrs. C., Jack, the prof, Perdita, Katherine, and Maggie. What roles do they play in the narrative? Do you think they assist or hinder Nadia's growth and repair? Explain.

4. Kephart uses flashbacks to powerful effect in the first half of the novel. What does each flashback contribute to the story? What do we learn about Nadia and her past? How are these memories significant in her present day life?

5. Discuss the role of perspective and point of view in this novel. How would the use of third person point of view change the story? What did the change to Maggie's perspective midway through the novel contribute to the narrative? How would the novel have been different if it had been narrated by Nadia to its conclusion?

6. Examine the stylistic differences between our two narrators' voices. What do these differences reveal about each character?

7. Kephart tells several stories within the novel, such as the story of Cimabue's Christ (pages 162–164) and Nadia's dream (pages 166–169). What role does each of these stories play in the larger narrative? Discuss the central theme of storytelling in *One Thing Stolen*.

8. Who—or what—is Benedetto?

9. The quote "Their one thing lost, their other thing gained" (page 192) applies to Nadia's experience with frontotemporal dementia. Explain how else this quotation might be applied to the story.

10. How do people survive even the most terrible of losses? What do you think? What answers does Kephart offer in this story?

11. Nadia is increasingly unable to express herself in spoken language. Challenge yourself to silence for a few hours, or even a day. Discuss your experience. When did you feel most compelled to speak, but could not? How did you feel? Now imagine that, like Nadia, you are not only unable to respond to others, but also to come up with the words to speak. What greater understanding do you now have of Nadia?

12. Beth Kephart begins her novel with the epigraph "There are 400 billion birds in this world. Every one of them came from an egg." After finishing the novel, discuss the meaning of this epigraph in the context of the story.

One Thing Stolen was born of Beth Kephart's obsession with birds, nests, rivers, and floods, as well as her deep curiosity about the mysteries of the human mind. It was in Florence, Italy, among winding streets and fearless artisans, that she learned the truth about the devastating flood of 1966, met a few of the Mud Angels who helped restore the city more than fifty years ago, and began to follow the trail of a story about tragedy and hope.

Beth is the award-winning author of nineteen books for readers of all ages, including *You Are My Only*, *Small Damages*, *Handling the Truth: On the Writing of Memoir*, and *Going Over*. She teaches creative nonfiction at the University of Pennsylvania, where a large portion of this novel is set.

Also by Beth Kephart:

★ "An excellent example of historical fiction focusing on an unusual time period." —*School Library Journal*, starred review

★ "A stark reminder of the power of hope, courage, and love." —*Booklist*, starred review

★ "Beautiful characters bring to light the power of love in its various facets." —Shelf Awareness, starred review

A Junior Library Guild selection